KELLY ANDREWS

WILLIAM POST

authorHOUSE®

AuthorHouse™
1663 Liberty Drive
Bloomington, IN 47403
www.authorhouse.com
Phone: 1 (800) 839-8640

Published by AuthorHouse 07/07/2017

ISBN: 978-1-5246-9884-3 (sc)
ISBN: 978-1-5246-9883-6 (e)

Print information available on the last page.

Any people depicted in stock imagery provided by Thinkstock are models,
and such images are being used for illustrative purposes only.
Certain stock imagery © Thinkstock.

This book is printed on acid-free paper.

Because of the dynamic nature of the Internet, any web addresses or links contained in
this book may have changed since publication and may no longer be valid. The views
expressed in this work are solely those of the author and do not necessarily reflect the views
of the publisher, and the publisher hereby disclaims any responsibility for them.

PREFACE

Like most of my stories, Kelly Andrews is a young man seeking his way through life. I wanted a sudden and startling beginning to the book, and think I achieved that. I seem to drift back to the Civil War in many of my novels, because the period after the Civil War was the dramatic time of the cowboy era.

The cowboy era only lasted about fifty years, but it was an indelible period because of the excitement. The law was sparse, and men from the war were broke, and without jobs. This caused many to turn to the outlaw trail. There were the James brothers, the Dalton brothers, the Younger brothers, Butch Cassidy and many others that were not as famous.

The renegade Indians were still prevalent throughout the West. Many people wanted to go to California or Oregon, so wagon trains formed.

The transcontinental railroad was completed in 1869. This was a dream of President Lincoln. He thought the completion of the transcontinental railroad was nearly as important as winning the war. He was briefed on the progress of the railroad until his untimely death in 1864. His successor, Andrew Johnson, was also convinced of the importance of it. So, the railroad played a vital part in the cowboy era.

Like most young men who survived the war, Kelly Andrews came out tired and haggard. He wanted to be alone, and away from people. He had seen the worst of the killing, and considered himself fortunate to have survived. He was able to achieve being away from folks by coming west, and securing a job as a cowboy, just south of Springfield, Missouri.

This worked for him, as he enjoyed the solace of the cowboys life. However, this ended after three years when the ranch owner sold out, and the next owner had his own crew. Kelly had saved his money, and this allowed him to travel west again, and see new country. He had just arrived in Coffeeville, Kansas, and went to the bank to break a twenty dollar gold piece, where this story begins.

Like the majority of my novels the story lasts about two hundred pages. I made the comment before about keeping my novels short. I don't want my books to become a project. They are meant to entertain you for a few evenings when television is so boring you want to throw something at it.

I edit my own books, and you may find errors. Just count that as a Postism. I built two guesthouses at my home in Las Vegas. The sealing of the drywall is surely not the best. A contractor friend of mine was observing the walls, and told me he could send one of his drywall finishers over, and he would make the walls look perfect. I told him not to bother, that people wouldn't believe I built it if he did that. My books are somewhat of the same order, so just overlook the errors, as I was educated as an engineer.

I hope you enjoy reading this book as much as I did writing it. When I write, I don't know what is coming next either, so it is just as exciting writing it as it is reading.

LIST OF CHAPTERS

CHAPTER 1

THE BANK ROBBERY

KELLY ANDREWS had just rode into the town of Coffeeville, and had intended to change a twenty dollar gold piece into smaller change for handier use. He was in a short line with a young woman and a man in front of him. The door of the bank slammed open. Three masked men came in, and shouted for everyone to get on the floor.

Kelly hit the floor, but covertly put his twenty dollar gold piece in his boot. The robbers were now busy collecting cash from the cash drawers, and one was now in the safe with a sack, getting the money there.

Kelly was lying next to a young woman, who was so scared she was shaking. Kelly put his hand over hers and whispered, "It will be over soon. Just lie still and everything will be alright in a minute or so."

The robber, who was keeping watch said, "Shut up down there!"

The woman began to cry, and Kelly squeezed her hand. She stopped crying, and just looked at him. She was taken with his black eyes and wavy black hair. The robber yelled, "Okay lover boy, get up and help your sweetheart up. You're going with us. They won't shoot if you two are with us."

Kelly stood and helped the young woman to her feet. The robbers then went out the door with Kelly and the woman in front of them. The sheriff was now there with two of his deputies.

One robber said, "If you shoot at us, we will kill the man and woman." The robbers took two horses, that were at the hitching rail for Kelly and the woman to ride. One of them was Kelly's horse. They then rode out at a fast gallop.

The sheriff said, "If we pursue them, they may kill Patty. I wonder who the man was with her?"

One of the men said, "He may be with the gang, and just acted like he was another hostage, so he could keep Patty under control."

"I don't know," said another, "They shoved him pretty hard toward the horses."

Another man shouted, "They took my horse!"

The sheriff said, "Whose horse was the male hostage on?" No one answered. The sheriff then said, "It must have been the hostages' own horse."

The man who had accused Kelly as being part of the gang said, "I've never seen that guy. Has anyone else ever seen him?" No one said anything, so he continued, "That probably means he was with them."

"Hold on there, Audie," the sheriff rebuffed, "You have no proof of that."

"Why was he in the bank then?"

"Let's go in the bank and find out." After interviewing two customers and the bank teller, they all said Kelly was just waiting in line, when the robbers came in. They said he was ordered to the floor with the others.

Audie said, "That doesn't mean he wasn't one of them. He was probably sent in ahead of time to case the joint."

"Then why was he ordered to lie down with the rest, and was then shoved toward his horse?" one of the deputies asked.

Audie didn't have an answer. What was galling him was that Patty was leaning on the stranger, and looked like she liked him. Audie had tried to befriend her, but she would have nothing to do with him. He then said, "Maybe she was in on the robbery, also."

The sheriff was irritated now, and said, "Maybe you were in on it, and are just trying to incriminate someone else. Maybe I should lock you up."

Audie then wheeled about, and left the bank. Sheriff Mann then interviewed the bank president,, who was trying to assess the extent of his loss.

***

After they had run their horses a half-mile out of town the leader, Bob Hendley, said, "Slow down, they're not following us."

Jed Blair said, "What are we going to do with these two, Bob?"

"I think we should keep them for at least one more day to insure our get away."

Harris said, "Then they will be able to identify us with our masks off. I think we should let them go here, and take our chances."

Bob said, "That makes sense, but I think we should tie them up, and leave them by the road. Someone will eventually find them."

Blair said, "They are such lovers, let's tie them up together facing one another."

"Do what you want to do, Jed. Just make sure you tie them securely."

Jed had a streak of meanness in him. He told Kelly to take his pants and shorts off.

Kelly said, "I won't do that in front of the lady."

Jed took out his knife and said, "If you want your sweetheart to have a nasty scar on her face, then keep your pants on. Kelly then took off his pants and underwear. Ned went through his pants, and found Kelly's wallet. Ned cursed, as there was only six dollars in it. He then threw the wallet away. He then tore the woman's dress off, and the bottom half of her bloomers, so that she was bare from the waist down. She was terribly embarrassed, but Kelly said, "Don't mind them, Ma'am, I respect you. Just bide your time, and they will be gone soon."

Jed tied them together securely with their arms about one another. Their faces touched as he had wound the rope about their necks. Their bare lower bodies were now meshed together with her legs around his. They were tied so tightly together, that Kelly wondered if their circulation would be cut off.

The woman cried and said, "What will my fiancé say, when they find us like this."

"Don't worry about that now, Ma'am. He'll just be glad to have you back unharmed."

The three robbers gathered Kelly's and the woman's clothing, and rode off with them, laughing. They were left under a tree by the side of the rode.

Bob said, "You should have made them take off all their clothes, Jed," and they all laughed.

***

There was no conversation for awhile then Patty said, "I've never seen you before, who are you?"

"I just rode in from Springfield. I was working for a rancher who sold out. The new owner had his own crew, so I decided to see some new country. I feel lucky that they didn't kill us. I thought they would."

Patty said, "We should at least exchange names. I'm Patty La Barr. My daddy owns a ranch east of town."

"I'm Kelly Andrews. We may be here for awhile like this."

Patty said, "I need to make a call of nature very badly, Mr. Andrews. What will I do?"

"The only thing you can do, Miss La Barr, just go. Just be glad we are still alive."

Patty said, "I am so embarrassed," and with that Kelly felt her warm urine running down his legs. He decided to go himself, as he knew sooner or later he would need to go, and it would be less embarrassing if they went at the same time.

Nothing was said for awhile, so Kelly thought Patty would feel better if she talked. He said, "Tell me about your fiancé, Miss La Barr."

It was a little difficult to talk as there faces were meshed together. She said, "His name his Lamar Bates. He is a deputy to Sheriff Mann. He's out of town taking a prisoner to Topeka, and has been gone a week. I hope he's gone when they find us. He's somewhat jealous, and this would really set him off."

Every time she talked her lips came over Kelly's. She laughed and said, "I've given you more kissed today, than I have Lamar the whole time he has been courting me."

"I don't have much experience with women. as I was in the war, and then hired on with Mr. Elmore for three years. Please forgive me if my tallywacker acts up. I'm not used to having a lady's bare body against me, so if it acts up, please know that I have no control over it at times, and I mean nothing by it."

"It seems to be acting up now. I will act like it is our little boy and reprimand him. Shall we give him a name? 'Tallywhaker' doesn't seem to fit him. How about Harold?"

"That's okay with me, Ma'am. It helps for you to understand. Harold is good most of the time, but he gets excited around you."

Kelly now had a full erection, and She laughed and said, "We are just like a married couple with a dissident child. I will always cherish this moment. After this I feel we can talk about anything. It may help me, when I marry Lamar. I am very shy, but now I seem to know everything about you, Mr. Andrews."

"Yes, me and our dissident child. He just doesn't want to mind."

Patty said, "Well, he seems strong, and has a mind of his own. If you don't mind me saying so, he gives me comfort to talk about him like he is our child. I'm surely glad daddy isn't here. He would laugh about this for a year. He finds humor in everything. If he were here, he would be in stitches listening to us. You'll see what I mean when you meet him."

"Please don't tell him about our child, Patty, Harold is just for us. We may never be able to tell anyone about this, but it is a comfort to have him with us. I don't feel nearly as embarrassed, now that you have accepted him. I just hope he doesn't spit up, as he is apt to do."

Patty really laughed then. She said, "Well, I have no way to clean him up if he does. Let's hope he is a good boy, and doesn't do that."

No one came the rest of the day. It was chilly that night, but their body heat kept them somewhat warm. Patty kissed Kelly off and on, and when she did Kelly lost control, and felt his reaction. She would laugh when Harold became excited, and it felt good to her.

She said, "Don't worry Mr. Andrews, I understand. Please forgive me, but I must go again. Kelly went at the same time. It was not nearly as embarrassing, as the first time.

***

Lamar came back to town late that night, and was told by the night jailor about Patty being taken by the outlaws. This was really upsetting to Lamar, and he went to Sheriff Mann's house, and woke him up. Mann told him what happened, and why they didn't pursue the robbers. He said, "I was afraid they may harm her if we went after them."

Lamar sat a minute and said, "You done the right thing, Sheriff. We'll follow them first thing in the morning, and see if they dropped them off along the way."

At the crack of dawn, the sheriff and Lamar were on the trail. They had not gone a mile until they found them. Lamar was shocked and mad. He shouted at Kelly, "Who are you, and why are you next to Patty like that? Have you no decency?"

The sheriff laughed at Lamar and said, "I don't think the man tied himself in that position, Lamar. He's probably as embarrassed about the situation as Patty. Untie them, Lamar, they have wet all over themselves."

Lamar was incensed and cut them loose. He said, "Cover yourself, Patty."

"With what, Lamar?"

"I don't know, but cover yourself."

Knowing nothing could be done the sheriff said, "You take Patty behind you, Lamar, and I'll take this man behind me. What's your name, Sir?"

"I'm Kelly Andrews, and I was just passing through town. I wanted to break a gold piece, and went to the bank to do so. Then the robbery occurred."

"That must be your wallet over their Mr. Andrews."

Kelly picked up his wallet, and immediately noticed his six dollars was gone. He said, "I guess I'm broke. Do you know anywhere I can get a job?"

Patty said, "My father will hire you, Mr. Andrews, at least until you are back on your feet."

"The hell he will," said Lamar. "I don't want you anywhere near that man. He's not fit company for you, and he's not to go to your ranch."

"So you are already giving me orders are you, Lamar? Mr. Andrews was a perfect gentleman, and treated me with more respect that you have."

"You call pissing all over you respect?"

Patty said, "Sheriff I would prefer to ride behind you."

Lamar said, "Well, I ain't carrying that dirtied man behind me."

Sheriff Mann was irritated by now and said, "You'll carry him if you want to remain my deputy."

With that Lamar kicked his horse in the flanks, and raced off toward town.

The sheriff said, "After I check you out, you may have a job as a deputy, as I see I have an opening."

Kelly just walked beside the sheriff's horse and Patty said, "I'll walk with Mr. Andrews. It wouldn't be proper for me to ride behind you in my present condition, Sheriff."

Kelly took off his shirt and said, "Use this Miss La Barr, I may as well be completely nude."

The first place they came to was Mrs. Arnold's house. She was a widow. The sheriff explained what had happened. Patty was given some slacks the woman had. She pointed to a room and said, "My late husband's clothes are still in the closet. He also has underwear in the top drawer of the dresser." She then asked if they were hungry, and both nodded. She said, "Sit down, and I will rustle you up some breakfast while you dress."

Sheriff Mann explained the circumstances, and how Lamar had reacted. He then said, "I'll go get my buckboard, and come get you in a bit."

Mrs. Arnold said, "You two seem to fit together. I never liked that Lamar. You are lucky you found out what kind of a man he was before you married him, Patty."

"Where are you from Mr. Andrews?"

For the past three years, I worked on a ranch near Springfield, but the owner sold out and the new owner had his own crew, so I decided to see some new country."

Mrs. Arnold said, "Well, it started off good for you here, being tied up to Patty all night. That seems a good way to get acquainted," and they all laughed.

***

When the sheriff returned with a buckboard, Patty said, "Come with me to the ranch, Mr. Andrews, I'm sure father can find something for you."

8

"If you don't mind, I think I will see if I can get employment with Sheriff Mann. I think he can teach me something more than being a cowpuncher."

"Well, if you ever want a job, you have one, as the offer will still be good."

In town when Patty parted from Kelly, she hugged him before she left. Kelly retrieved his twenty dollar gold piece from his boot, and went into the bank to get it changed. Audie Bell was in the bank and yelled, "The robbers are back!"

The teller said, "Forgive Mr. Bell, he seems to think everyone he meets is a robber now. How may I help you?"

"I need to break this twenty dollar gold piece into smaller denominations. I prefer folding money."

As Kelly was leaving he said to Bell, "I think the sheriff is investigating you, Mr. Bell, as an accessory to robbery. I would watch my step if I were you. Some of the townspeople may not want to wait for a trial."

Bell's eyes grew and said, "Why would he investigate me?"

Kelly said, "I asked myself that same question when you accused me?"

Kelly walked down to the sheriff's office. He asked if he could be put on as a deputy on an interim basis, while he was being checked out."

"I'll do that Mr. Andrews. Please sit down, and write out what you've been doing the past five years."

"I was in the army for four years prior to my job punching cows. I was in the cavalry. I am really lucky to be alive. I learned to use a gun fairly well then, but hope to only use it rarely, now.

"I got a job after the war punching cows on a ranch near Springfield. You can reach my boss, Mr. Elmore, by just writing to the Post Office in Springfield. They all know him, as he is a councilman there. He told me he was going to build a house in town, and retire from the cattle business."

The sheriff posted a letter that day to Councilman Elmore. The sheriff went over Kelly's duties. He would come on duty at six in the afternoon. He would then have rounds to make every four hours, until six in the morning. He would have Sunday's off, unless they had prisoners in the jail.

Sheriff Mann said, "I would like you to go with me when I'm investigating a crime. You can then see how I handle things."

"Sheriff, I would like to go after those bank robbers if you'll let me. I think I can identify them by there voices."

"Yes, but they will be able to identify you on sight. Wouldn't that be dangerous?"

"Maybe, but I plan on wearing a beard and mustache and a different kind of hat. That may throw them off, as they only saw me that one time, and most of that time they were looking at Miss La Barr."

"Where would you look, Kelly?"

"I'll start with the towns that are close. They seemed to know the layout around here pretty well. They could live quite close."

"I think you may be right. I don't think they were any of the notorious gangs, like the James brothers or the Younger gang. The James brothers are two and the Younger's are many. No, I think they're probably within a hundred miles. Why don't you check out Joplin. Check in with the sheriff, and tell him you are working undercover for me. I'll write you a letter. I know the sheriff there. He's Erdie Wulfgen. He's an honest man, and honest men are fewer since the war.

"I only have a budget for your pay, so I can't pay for your expenses. However, if you apprehend the robbers and recover some of the money, I'm sure there will be a substantial reward put up by the bank. I'm not going to tell anyone you are my deputy, except the town council when they are in executive session, and I'll tell them to keep quiet about you. That way, no one can tip off the robbers, if there is anyone there who knows them."

Kelly laughed and said, "Have Audie Bell write down where he's been for the last few month."

Sheriff Mann laughed and said, "I'll do that, Kelly. I'll do it in front of others, and ask the others if Bell has been spending more money lately."

Kelly laughed, then said, "You will have to furnish me a horse as my horse was stolen."

The sheriff laughed and said, "Now I see why you are so eager to find the robbers."

"They also took three hundred dollars from me that was hidden under my saddle in a secret pouch."

"Please do me a favor, before you leave for Joplin, drop by the La Barr ranch and meet Patty's father. It's practically on your way. It will mean a lot to Leland and Patty."

"You're right, Sheriff. That would be the gentlemanly thing to do."

***

As Kelly rode up to the La Barr ranch, La Barr was just coming out the front door. He yelled back inside, "Patty we have company."

Patty came out the door wiping her hands on a tea towel. She then saw Kelly getting off his horse. She said, "Daddy, this is Mr. Andrews, the fellow I was tied up to all night."

La Barr stepped forward and said, I'm Leland La Barr and shook Kelly's hand. He then said, "Are you coming to make an honest woman out of Patty?"

"Daddy! Please forgive my father, he makes a joke out of everything. He was really pleased to hear I broke up with Lamar."

La Barr said, "Patty told me of the circumstances of your trials."

"They weren't all bad, Mr. La Barr. Patty is a beautiful woman."

"She is that. Looks just like her ma, bless her soul. I hope to see you around here some. Patty told me what a gentleman you were to her."

11

"I came to tell you I will be out of town for a spell. I've been hired to look in on some things for a man."

"How long will you be gone, Mr. Andrews?" Patty asked.

"I wish I could say, but I just don't know. However, when I return, I will stop here before I go to town."

"Then, you're making Coffeyville your home for now?" asked Patty.

"Of course I am. After spending the night with you, I can't just walk away."

Patty smiled broadly and said, "We do have a bond now, don't we?"

"Bring a ring when you come, Mr. Andrews. I like short courtships," mused La Barr.

"Just forgive him Mr. Andrews. He'll never change."

"Please call me Kelly, Kelly Andrews."

"I prefer to call you Kelly. You must call me, Patty."

"Yes, you two should be on a first name basis by now. I'll just call you, Son," and La Barr laughed as he was leaving for the barn.

Patty said, "Please have a cup of coffee with me, Kelly, before you go. I need to know you better, before daddy marries us off."

Kelly said, "Sounds good to me."

Over coffee each told a brief history of themselves. Kelly then said, "I've got to be on my way. I have a long ride ahead of me."

"If you're gone for more than two weeks, write me a letter? Just put my name on it, and Coffeyville. I'll get it."

"Okay." Kelly stood up and Patty came into his arms and kissed him a long kiss."

"She said, "That will have to do you for now."

As Kelly rode away he thought, "*What have I gotten myself into. I was just minding my own business then whamo! I have a person who wants to marry me.*"

CHAPTER 2

JOPLIN

Kelly had to spend one night on the trail, but reached Joplin a day later. He went directly to Sheriff Wulfgen's office, showed him his badge, and handed him the letter Sheriff Mann had written. After Wulfgen read it, he said, "Deputy, I will help you all I can. This town is a lot wilder now, than before the war. A lot of men are without jobs, and some of them are outlaws.

"I have an idea. Tonight, I will come into Hall's saloon, and arrest you. You don't have a place to stay tonight anyway. I will tell them that I have a wanted poster on you for armed robbery. Tomorrow, I will let you out, and say that the warrant had been dropped for lack of evidence.

"Then that night, be in the saloon. I'll drop by and tell you that I'm keeping an eye out for you as I have heard rumors about you. If there is any criminal element around, they may want you to help them in their criminal endeavors."

"In the meantime, Sheriff, no one, who is a decent person, will have anything to do with me."

"See, I'll be savin' you a lot of useless talk."

Kelly smiled and said, "I see your point."

It went off just as the sheriff said. Wufgen handcuffed Kelly and took him off to jail. The saloon was crowded when the arrest was made. It got real quiet, and everyone saw Kelly being cuffed.

The next night Kelly was in the saloon. He stood alone, and no one came near him. A saloon girl, who was older than the other girls, came up to him and said, "I watched you standing alone as if you had lost your last friend. I love your black eyes, you're handsome enough, and just to show you that this town is friendly, I'm going to buy you a drink."

Kelly smiled at her and said, "You're a sight for sore eyes. What's your name?"

"I'm Betty Kelly. What's your name? My name is Kelly, too. However, that's my first name."

"We're practically married having the same name. Are you as bad as the sheriff says?"

"I'm no choir boy, but I've never been convicted of a crime."

About that time the sheriff came in, and everything got quiet. He came up to Kelly, and said his piece about keeping an eye on him.

Kelly said, "Sheriff, you've made these people think I'm a criminal."

Wulfgen said, "If the shoe fits….and I think I have your size." He then turned to Betty and said, "You're known by the company you keep, Betty," and left.

After he had gone, Betty kissed him on the check and said, "Cheer up, Kelly, the night is young, and I like you. Do you have a room for the night?"

Kelly said, "Not yet."

She said, "We have an extra room in the attic that we keep for emergencies. You can use that, until you make other arrangements. I hope you will stick around for awhile."

She winked at him, and started to walk away, when Kelly said, "What will I do if the owner comes around?"

"Just move over to the other side of the bed, I'm the owner."

Kelly was shocked, but tried not to show it.

Several days passed, and people began to warm up a little to Kelly. Betty was always glad to see him. Kelly bought a drink for an old timer, then asked about Betty. The old timer said, "Betty, she and her husband bought this saloon some two years ago. He was an older man, and about six months ago he died of a heart attack. I can see why, Betty gets anyone's heart beatin' faster than it should. She surely likes you, I see. She don't mix much with the young customers. Her girls do all the flirtin'. You're the first I've seen that she cottoned to."

"I think she felt sorry for me, as the sheriff made it hard for anyone to like me He thinks I'm a crook, and let everyone know what he thinks."

"Well, Sonny, are you a crook?"

"I did some bad things during the war, but then that was war. I've kept my nose clean since then."

"You weren't with the *Red Legs* were you?"

"No, Mosby."

"Oh, well, he wasn't as bad as them *Red Legs*"

Every night Betty would talk to Kelly. She had a voice that was soft, and Kelly really like to hear her talk. She said, "I met him in Saint Louis. He was an older man, but was young for his age. He told me if I would go with him to Joplin, he would sell his saloon in Saint Louis and put my name on the deed of the saloon in Joplin. I liked that, and although I wasn't that much in love with him, I came with him.

"I was married before that. We were together for six years, but the war took him. Brian gave me a job and treated me decent. I didn't have to sell myself for a living like I thought I would. He taught me the business from the ground up. He was a smart man, and had patience teaching me the bookwork, and how to handle the saloon. I also learned how to handle the girls.

"I'm a bit too old for you, Kelly, but I like you. I haven't been with a man since Brian died. I didn't think I needed a man until I met you. You seemed to bring the desire back. I think it was how you stood by yourself, that pulled my heart stings. I was homeless and friendless after my first husband was killed. I remembered what it was like. Seeing you standing there alone, I felt I must reach out to you. Now, you have become dear to me."

Another week went by, but one night Kelly was awakened by his door opening. Before he could reach his gun Betty slid in beside him. Nothing was said, but they made love most of the night. When he woke the next morning, she was gone. He began thinking. *"What if it wasn't Betty. What if she just sent one of her girls."* He was really worried then.

He came downstairs and Betty was making coffee. She smiled and said, "Are you sorry?"

"No, are you.?"

"No, I'm happier than I've been since I married my first husband. You are more open than he was, and I know you better. Will you stick around awhile?"

"It may be hard for you to believe, but I'm on a job. I can't tell you what it's about, but just trust me, I'm not an outlaw."

"I know that. I am curious what you are about, though."

"It shouldn't be too long before I can tell you. Will you come back to see me again, or was that a one night stand?"

"You surely have a way of turning things around, Kelly. I'm not just using you." She paused then, and said, "I guess in a way I am. I like the way you make love."

Things seemed to not be going anywhere, so Kelly went to the local bank. He asked to speak with the president. He was shown into Charlie Thompson's office. Kelly asked, "May I speak to you in confidence, Mr. Thompson?"

Thompson leaned toward Kelly and said, "What about?"

"I'm on a case, and I want to know if any person has made a large deposit lately?"

"I'm not allowed to disclose records of the bank to anyone, but if you are a law officer, I will help you."

Kelly showed him his badge and said, "Please, never reveal I'm a law officer or it could get me killed."

"I will of course never mention it to anyone. I have been worried about my own bank, since the bank in Coffeyville was robbed. I take it you are on that case."

Kelly nodded. Thompson then said, "No one has made any deposits that are unusual."

Thompson then said, "I have read that most banks are robbed near the end of the day. That way, there is more money, and the robbers will have the darkness to cover their trail. It is also known that a large shipment of cash is coming in Friday, as an army column is bivouacked near here, and the army is paying off their troops, Monday.

I'll pay you ten dollars if you will spend the afternoon in my vault. I will keep it ajar so if there is a robbery, they will go into the safe. You will be waiting for them if someone comes."

"This seems to me like a job for your sheriff or one of his deputies."

"Yes, I suppose it is, but Erdie is sixty-five, and his deputy is so slow I know he would be killed."

"Yes, I expect he would. If there are several robbers, most men, no matter how talented they are, would be killed. I think a safer place is across the street. I will wait there. I will know if the bank is being robbed, and be able to shoot at them from a safe vantage point."

Friday was the next day and Kelly found himself a safe place behind a large wooden box that was directly across from the bank. Near four that afternoon, three riders rode up, and tied their horses right in front of Kelly. One of the horses was his horse.

As the men left for the bank, Kelly took the three horses, and led them down the street to an alley, and then down the alley to a corral. He then returned. He had just got behind the box, as the robbers were coming out of the bank. They looked for their horses and from behind box Kelly said, "The sheriff took your horses. You can give up or be gunned down. It's your choice."

One of the men raised his gun, and Kelly shot him dead. The other two dropped their guns and raised their hands. Someone had gone for the sheriff. Moments later, he came running up with his deputy following him. He was panting so hard he couldn't talk. He did have his gun out, and took the robbers into custody. Kelly gathered the money, and took it back to the bank. He was met by Charlie Thompson, who lauded him profusely. When they sat down, Charlie said, "Thank you deputy Andrews, There will be a hundred dollars deposited in your name at the bank of Coffeyville."

"Thanks Mr. Thompson, I appreciate it. I need to go to the sheriff's office now."

Sheriff Wulfgen was ecstatic. Kelly then told him about the horses. and that one of them was his.

The sheriff said, "For helping us out, I will give you a bill of sale for the other two horses. This will make my re-election. I'll give you all the credit, though."

"No, use it for your election, Sheriff. I certainly don't care. You did arrest them." This brought a large smile to the sheriff's face and he said, "Thanks a lot, Deputy. I am truly grateful."

Kelly brought the horses around, and looked in their saddle bags. There were bills of sales for both horses, and his bill of sale was in the saddle bag, but his name had been crossed out. He brought all three bills of sale into the sheriff. He issued new bills of sale for all three, and put them in Kelly's name. His three hundred dollars was still in the pouch under his saddle.

***

Unbeknown to Kelly, the U. S. Marshall for the territory was visiting Sheriff Mann. Sheriff Mann had just received a wire from Sheriff Wulfgen telling how Kelly had brought down the gang who robbed both banks. The prosecutor was now working on a deal with the robbers to get the money back from the Coffeyville bank robbery for a lighter sentence.

Mann was lauding the work of his deputy to U. S. Marshall Lou Dobbs. He told Dobbs how smart the deputy was. What Mann didn't know was that Dobbs was looking for a man for a covert assignment, and Kelly Andrews appeared to be a perfect fit.

When Kelly returned to Coffeyville, Dobbs decided to approach Andrews and buy him supper. He had been authorized to pay Andrews a hundred dollars up front, if he could infiltrate the Farwell Company. He was then to await further information that would be furnished by another operative with the code word, "blue crow."

The operative would then pay him another hundred, and give him further instructions. However, Dobbs must convince him to take the assignment. Dobbs would receive a bonus of fifty dollars from the attorney general's office if the new operative worked out.

The new man was to go to Topeka, and infiltrate a group there who had come from New York. It was a company that operated openly, because everything they did appeared to be lawful. However, Dobbs had been told by an assistant to the attorney general, that they had shady dealings. They just needed a man on the inside, so he could bring charges against them.

What Marshal Dobbs didn't know was that this was a sham company set up by the federal government. Only a handful of people knew of its existence, and they were in Washington DC. The marshal had just been instructed to recruit highly talented men.

The head of the company was Louis Farwell. He had bought a mansion in Topeka, and lived an opulent lifestyle.

Sheriff Dobbs knew he must hire a clever man, who could get the goods on Farwell, expose him and jail him. Dobbs wanted to bring down Farwell to further his career. He also wanted the fifty dollar bonus.

Dobbs knew the job was probably risky. He had sent a good man, Charles Letford, to investigate, but Letford returned several weeks later and resigned. He would not say why. Dobbs took it, that Farwell or his associates, had frightened him into silence. Dobbs had let some of his colleagues know his intentions with Letford. This got him to thinking that Farwell may had gotten to someone in his own organization. He then decided to keep silent about the next person he sent. He would tell people, that his new deputy was being lent to the army, and would be out of the country for a year or so.

***

Kelly stopped off to see Patty on his way back, but she was away tending to a sick aunt. He saw Leland and told him he was back, then went on to town. He had been given the recovered Coffeeville's bank money, and had it with him. Just a little over a hundred was missing. The bank was elated to get back the lion share of their stolen money.

Kelly had just checked into a hotel for the night. He had cleaned up, and was about to go to dinner, when he heard a knock at his door. It was U. S. Marshal Dobbs. Kelly explained that he was going to dinner, and Dobbs said, "I need to talk to you, but we can do it over dinner on the government's dime."

Kelly agreed to that. They stayed at the table over an hour, as Dobbs laid out his proposition. He also told Kelly that he would be paid expenses, so he had to keep track of that in order to be paid. Dobbs added that he needed to live large, to make an impression. As few people knew Kelly in this area, Dobbs thought Kelly was the perfect choice. If Kelly took the job, Dobbs decided to write Sheriff Wulfgen, and ask him not to talk about Kelly, as he had hired him for a special job.

At dinner Kelly said, "It sounds good, Marshal Dobbs, but I will have to think about it. I have a girlfriend here. That may come to an end if I take the job. She is only nineteen and may wait a year for me. If she doesn't, then I would like to know that, also."

The next day Kelly went to see Patty. She was glad to see him, but said, "You didn't write. I took it that you didn't want to keep seeing me. I would like to talk more, but Richard Thomas is coming to pick me up and take me to the County Fair."

Kelly said, "I couldn't write, Patty. Circumstances in my undercover operation prevented me from doing so. I wanted to tell you that I have been offered another job that is out of town. I will be gone for over a year, this time. It is a long time to wait, but there it is. I can't tell you anymore, as it is a covert operation. You will just have to take me on faith. I will surely understand if you want to go out with other guys while I'm gone. I'm not sure everything would work out for us anyway. It will be mostly up to you."

Patty said, "When we were together all night, I had very warm feelings toward you. However, your occupation has seemed to put a barrier between us. When we were tied together, there was nothing between us. I will have to sort this out. I can't promise anything, as I know you can't. Let's just leave it at that. What every will be, will be.

"I do want to kiss you goodbye. I want more than that, but that would be sinful. Just keep that in mind, and it may bring you back to me. If things work out, I will be waiting, but I may find someone else, only God knows. Will you be in harm's way?"

Kelly nodded and said, "I might not be back at all. However, after this job, I will not take another assignment like this one, if you wait for me. My, how our lives are complicated. It used to be so easy. I would get up, put in twelve good hours of work, then fall into bed after supper with nothing on my mind. Now it takes me hours to go to sleep, as there are dozens of things to think about.

"Don't feel guilty about dating other men. I met a girl in Joplin that wanted me. We had a small relationship, and that was good, because I could then see you were the one. I will probably have to see other women on my next assignment, as they always seem to work into the scheme of things. However, that is just part of the job. There is little, if any, romance to it."

"That does make it better. If we are both cheating on one another, it's better," and they both laughed. "I won't tell daddy, he would make a mountain out of a mole hill. He's still not over us being tied up all night together nearly nude. He gets a kick out of the darnedest things. He would really like this one."

"Then tell him, but tell him he can't share it with anyone but you, or your reputation will be tarnished."

"I may do that, as he gets such a kick out of my love life. To me it's sad, but to him it's the funniest thing in the world. If I marry anyone but you, he will tell my husband all these things, and my husband may run off."

"Well, that's another reason for telling him." Patty kissed him again and this time Kelly had to pull away again. He said, "You've got Harold acting up again, Patty. Seems you always have your way with him," and they both laughed. Kelly then said, "Please don't tell your dad about that," and they both died laughing.

Kelly could see a cloud of dust in the distance. He said, "That will be your beau. I'll leave by another way. I don't want to spoil your evening."

Patty said, "I will think of you and Harold, Kelly," and they laughed as Kelly rode away.

CHAPTER 3

TOPEKA AND THE TRAINING

In Topeka, Kelly registered at a hotel near a huge sign that said: THE FAREWELL COMPANY. His room had a water closet with a four footed bathtub. Kelly had noticed the hotel dinning room, as he checked in. His stomach was growling by the time he entered the dining room. He could see a portion of the dining room was roped off, and he could see several men and women dining in that area.

Kelly was greeted by a waiter who seated him. Kelly asked, "Who are those people?"

"That is Mr. Farwell and his party. They dine here nearly every evening."

"What does Mr. Farwell do?"

"He runs the Farwell Company and everything else he wants to."

"You don't sound like you like Mr. Farwell much."

The waiter made a face and said, "Before Mr. Farwell arrived, we were a peaceful little village. He has brought a lot of business to Topeka, but along with it a lot of people."

"Is Mr. Farwell a bad person?"

"I wouldn't say he's bad, but a lot of bad things happened after his company and its subsidiaries arrived. My family and I are religious, and are opposed to some of the things that the Farwell company does."

"Like what?"

"I've said too much already. Please excuse my bad manners, Sir."

"I find you very interesting, and would like to know you better. My name is Kelly Andrews. What is your name?"

"My name is August Mining. Did you know you are the first person to ask my name in the three years I've worked here?"

"Well, that's a shame Mr. Mining. I find that people like you are the people who make this country great. I admire you for putting your religion first. God blessed us by letting us live in America. I was in the war, and it brought home to me how great our country is. I prayed a lot during the war, and God brought me through it, when all odds were against that happening."

"I see you are a religious man, also, Mr. Andrews."

"Just Kelly, please. Many of my colleagues became religious, also, when the cannon balls were raining down on us. I try to put it behind me, but it is no use. I dream every night about the war, and sometimes wakeup with sweat running off me, as if I were sitting out in the Kansas sun in July."

"I wasn't in the war, but I prayed for men like you every night. I thank you for your service. Were you on the side of the Union?"

"It really doesn't matter what side anyone was on, now."

"I guess you're right. I'm glad I got to talk with you. I will always count you as a friend. I will invite you to our church. It's not big. It was founded by a friend of John Wesley. I got to hear Reverend Wesley preach once. I counted that as a great honor."

"Why is that, Mr. Mining?"

"Because he loves our Savior so much, that he seemed to glow."

"My, I would like to meet the man someday."

"What will you have, Kelley? I will suggest our steak tonight. It was a yearling and the meat is tender. It comes with mashed potatoes and gravy. After you taste Stu's gravy you will come back for more.

"Then bring it on, Mr. Mining."

"Please call me August, now that we are friends."

The meal was as good as August said it was. Kelly asked August if he could meet the cook. August took him back and Kelly said, "After tasting your gravy, I had to meet you. I'm Kelly Andrews," and extended his hand.

The cook took his hand, and put his other hand over their clasped hands and said, "I'm Stuart Blinn. It is very rare that someone comes back to complement my cooking."

"Well, people might not come back here, but they are all thinking about you and your marvelous talent."

"I invited Mr. Andrews to our church, Stu."

"I hope you will come, Mr. Andrews. We preach from the Bible, and honor our Lord Jesus."

"Sounds like where I should be."

The next day Kelly went to the Farwell company, and asked about employment. The office clerk asked his name and the clerk said, "We have been expecting you, Mr. Andrews."

This shocked Kelly. He said, "How did you know I was coming here? I didn't even know myself until yesterday."

"Mr. Farwell will tell you that," as he led Kelly into Mr. Farwell's office. He knocked on Farwell's door, and a voice said, "Come in."

The clerk said, "This is Mr. Kelly Andrews, Mr. Farwell."

Farwell said, "Have a seat Mr. Andrews," and the clerk left.

Farwell smiled and said, "Sheriff Dobbs wired the attorney general about hiring you. The A. G. then wired me you were coming. Dobbs said he recruited you to do a special job. I bet he told you that my company was doing a lot of shady business, and you were to investigate us?"

Kelly was further shocked and said, "Yes, how would you know that?"

"Because the sheriff is just part of a larger plan. He was told to recruit talented men, who can work under cover and get vital information. I am under contract with the federal government to recruit men like you for special missions. If you accept a position with us, you will go through a yearlong training program, that will put you in a position to accomplish a special job. The training is very difficult, and only a few make it through. If you are willing to do this training, you will swear an oath to the United States, that you will never reveal your training or any part of the assignments we may have for you. Many leave, but we have never heard anyone of the ones who left, say a word about us. All are loyal to the United States, and hold it sacred, as you do."

"How would you know that?" Kelly asked.

After Sheriff Dobbs sent us your name, we did a little investigating. We found you served in the war. Your war record showed you served admirably for four years even though with the Rebels. You served with Colonel Mosby, who is now working for our government. You were decorated for your valor, and were an inspiration to the men who served under you."

"That was more luck than anything. Many men, who were much better than me, died in that cause. Please let me know what I am getting into. It seems like a secret organization, and I despise secret organizations. I believe a government should be open to its citizens."

"I agree, but there is always organizations that are conspiring to do harm to the citizens of this country. That is why we have to do something to stem what they are doing. We want to root out these people, and bring them to justice, like you did those bank robbers in Joplin.

"You are just the type of person we are looking for. As the training goes on, you will understand much more. With your allegiance to your country, you will want to help preserve her."

"What is the organization called, Mr. Farwell?"

"We have no name. I, and my company, aid the United States of America. I have a contract to find young men and interview them. If you agree, you will be sent by rail to a place near Washington DC to go through a training course that will last several months. You will be paid by the government, fifty dollars a month and your expenses, while you are in training. After that, the government will assign you to an area where you will be used. They, at that time, will negotiate a pay scale commensurate with the danger of the activity you will be assigned to stop. I have heard that it could be a lump sum or a weekly wage. Are you still interested?"

"Yes, I have nothing to lose, and the training could be useful to me later in life, whether I stay with them or not."

Kelly boarded a train for Washington DC and was there two days later. He met with an army colonel named Colonel Alfred. The colonel interviewed him again. He then laid out the training program he was to go through.

Colonel Alfred said, "If you make it through the training, you will become a United States Marshal. You will not have a district, as you will be working in various parts of the country. Your title will be United States Marshal at Large. Meaning you have the same status as any of the U. S. Marshals. Your base pay will be that of a U. S. Marshall. However, we'll give you a bonus, based on the type of job you are asked to do.

The more risky the job, the more pay. Your pay is generally a lump sum for the job, plus expenses of course.

After asking about the same questions that Farwell asked, Kelly was given an address near the town of Langley, Virginia. They had a training facility, but no living facilities. He would have to find that for himself. He read the paper, and saw an advertisement of a room above a gunsmith's business.

The gunsmith, Howard Tart, asked what business he was in. Kelly told him he worked for the federal government in personnel. This satisfied Tart, and he gave him the price, then said, "If you want to reduce your rent, I need an assistant at night sometimes and don't like to pay a fulltime wage."

Kelly said, "I'm interested. I would like to learn something about your trade, as it may come in handy someday."

The training at Langley was intense. They started at seven in the morning, and went until noon in a classroom. Then after a half-hour lunch, they had physical training. The physical training was done by two Japanese men. Both were stoutly built. They did a different type of fighting, where they used the leverage of their opponent to their advantage. It required quick reflex action. Kelly was very apt at learning this, as he was very quick. Although he could best his other five classmates, he was not even a challenge for the two Japanese men. However, as the class went on, he became better and better. It pleased his instructors, and they spent extra time with him. After six months, he was becoming a challenge, and the instructors fought with him a lot.

The classroom consisted of learning to observe things around them in minute detail. They learned to evaluate people by their habits. They were taught how to manipulate people by asking questions that seemed innocuous, but could get the information they desired.

Women were brought into their training. They were taught the nuances of making a woman feel loved. The instructor said, "Always treat the woman, who you want information from, as an object of what you need to get from her. Do your best not to get involved with them, as they may be using you, the same way you want to use them."

One of the men said, "Are we to make love to these women?"

"Not if you can get out of it. Intimacy brings on what you never want to do, that is love the person you are using. Just think of this as part of the job. I know it will be difficult sometimes, but you never know when you are being used. If you are to be an excellent agent, you must guard against any feelings for the woman you are trying to extract information from.

Kelly thought the women who helped train them, must be professionals in that trade, as they were very seductive, and showed them ways to bring a woman under their spell. One of the women, who was training Kelly said, "It's hard not to get involved. You give me feelings that I have not felt with others."

Kelly said, "That is what I am trying to do, Tracy. I want you to love me dearly. She smiled and said, "You're doing too good of a job, as I want you badly. Could we meet at night sometimes?"

Kelly said, "Of course, I will ask my wife to fix dinner for you?"

Tracy was shocked and said, "I thought you had to be single to be in this service."

"You do, Tracy, I was just pulling your chain, so we didn't get involved. You do the same to me, but I know we can't be involved."

They also were taught to pick pockets. There was a man and his wife who were experts at this. One would pick the pocket, then pass the articles to the other. It was so smooth, that none of the trainees could see the exchange. Demonstrations were given, and each of the men in Kelly's class, and him, were amazed that after just a few minutes the couple had extracted both their wallets and watches. None of the men were aware of them taking these items. This class was for an hour each day and lasted the entire time of their training. Kelly became very smooth. One of the men said, "If this job doesn't work out, then we will have a trade to fall back on," and the whole class laughed.

Another part of their training was playing poker. The leader said, "Every place you go, there are card games. We have a man who can teach you the nuances of playing, so you will be an expert."

This training also went on for months. The man training them was Joe Brown. He explained that he made his living from gambling, but in his latter years, he didn't want the stress anymore. He first showed them the way crooked gamblers would try to cheat them. Each man became astute at spotting a "second card" deal, dealing from the bottom and many other ploys of cheaters. There was also a way to cheat by bringing in a new deck. When that happened, Joe showed them how to cut the cards so the dealer would not get the hand he thought.

Joe taught them to read the players mannerisms. If you studied the mannerisms, you could sometimes tell whether your opponent had a good hand, a medium hand or was bluffing. Joe could mimic these mannerisms, so the men could get the idea.

Joe said, "I have a method that kept me out of a lot of trouble. If you win too often the other players will think you are cheating. So, I never deal. I explain that if I never deal, I can never be accused of cheating, because that is where ninety percent of the cheating is done." They were also taught how to palm cards to be used if they needed to cheat. Kelly was extremely good at this as his hands were large.

All the men became masters at playing poker. Luck had something to do with it, but knowing the percentages of a hand and reading the mannerisms of the players were paramount to winning.

Joe also explained how to bet. How to lure men into betting when they shouldn't and how to fold your hand when you thought they were being cheated.

Joe said, "If someone accuses you of cheating, ask why he thought that. The answer will always be, 'you win too easily.' You can then tell the man you will stop playing with him, if he thinks you are a cheat. Try to defuse the situation by engaging other players. If the man is too hostile, simply push the pot of that hand towards him, and tell him that you are leaving before things get out of hand. Even then, you may be accosted. That is where you produce the derringer you have up your sleeve."

They were taught to shoot. First with a rifle then a handgun. Their boots were sewn where they could keep a derringer inside one of the boots. They were taught with a handgun how to pull and use it. The instructor said, "One thing you must bear in mind, it is not how fast you are, but how accurate you are. Never let quickness get in the way of accuracy."

He then asked, "How many of you have killed a man. Each man raised his hand. Kelly then knew that these men were hand picked. It seemed each man was better at one of their activities than the others. Kelly was better at hand-to-hand fighting than the others, but Mark Evers could draw his handgun faster than all of them. However, he would miss once in awhile. Kelly never missed.

With a rifle, all were about equal. All became superb marksmen. They were taught how to use a fifty caliber Sharps rifle with a scope that could hit something a half-mile away.

By the sixth month, three were dropped from the class. However, the three that stayed seemed to be apt.

At night Kelly helped the gunsmith. As they were working one night, Kelly asked, "I wonder if a man could make something to go on the end of his gun to make it practically silent?"

Howard said, "It's funny you would ask that. I have been thinking the same thing. I know that a gun takes all the air out of the barrel when it's fired. That creates a vacuum. That is the reason for the noise. If we could devise something that would screw onto the end of the barrel that had vents in it, the gas could escape gradually and then maybe make the gun quieter."

They began working on this project. Howard knew how to cut threads at the end of a barrel and then made a pipe that could screw on to the barrel. It was the same bore as the gun, but had vents cut into it. It took over a week to develop one for a handgun. It worked. Although there was some noise, it was much quieter. They then worked on a fifty-caliber Sharps, and it worked the same.

Howard said, "Don't tell anyone about this. I think we can get a patent and make a lot of money."

Kelly said, "You did all the work, Howard. You should just put it in your name. Besides, it may be easier with just one name."

Howard said, "Okay, but if I make a lot of money from this, I will insist on sharing it with you."

The training went on for nearly a year. By the eleventh month Kelly was the only one left in the class. He didn't know if the men who dropped out were asked to leave or did so on their own. What he did know was that he was very skilled now. He knew each person in his class, but never mixed with them.

When there were just two of them left, Warren McKay asked, "Why don't you mix with us?

Kelly said, "Warren, I work at night with a gunsmith learning that trade. It's as fascinating as this training. I feel I have learned more this year than all the other years of my life."

Warren said, "I do too, but sometimes I think that this could be something I shouldn't do. I'm thinking of dropping out. Most of the things we have learned are either illegal or unethical. I'm not sure I want to ever use any of this stuff. Just think what kind of a person you will be, if you do use this stuff on other people."

This philosophy got Kelly to thinking. McKay was right. What kind of person would he become. He decided to talk to Colonel Alfred about it, and traveled into Washington DC.

Colonel Alfred said, "You need to look at the big picture, Kelly. Just think how much better America will be by employing your skills on bad people."

On his way back to Langley, Kelly thought, "Colonel *Alfred is right. Someone has to do it, and they have spent a lot of time and money on me. I will continue and evaluate each job I am asked to do.*"

He thought about all the training, and especially the girls. *"I was such a rube with women. If I ever do have a lasting relationship, I can please my woman much better."*

Near the end of their training Kelly was brought to Washington for a meeting with Colonel Alfred. He said, "Kelly, at the end of training, each man is given a two week leave before he's given an assignment. In your case, I can't spare you. We have an agent who was sent to Pueblo, Colorado to look into the activities of a rancher. The rancher is said to own the town, and does anything he pleases. We learned this from a letter sent to the attorney general from a merchant, and two of the other merchants signed the letter.

"When we send a marshal into the field, he is required to write a postcard to his mother every three or four day. We are his mother, so if the postcards stop, we know he is in trouble. Lenard Valdez is the marshal we sent to Pueblo. We sent him, as he is Hispanic, and most of the people in Pueblo are Hispanics. We want you to leave on a train tonight and travel to Cheyenne, then on down to Denver. You will have to go by horse then. You should be there in three to four days at the most. Find out what happened to Marshal Valdez and advise us by post card if you feel you can handle the situation. If you can't, write a letter explaining why you need our help.

"Money will be wired to the Pueblo bank in your name. It will have your name on it, like you sent the money. Here is your badge and credentials, congratulations, you are now a United States Marshal at large."

CHAPTER 4

THE ASSIGNMENT

Kelly rode the train to Denver, then bought a fine horse. He used one of the postcards given him to write Patty La Barr. He said that he had not written because it was not allowed. He said he was now on an assignment that shouldn't last very long. He would then come to Coffeeville. The card showed no return address, but from the stamp of the post office, Patty could tell it was mailed from Denver.

Kelly had taken his fifty caliber Sharps, with the silencer that could be screwed on the barrel. His handgun also had a silencer. He outfitted himself, and began his journey. He decided not to follow the main trail, as he wanted to see some of the country next to the Rocky Mountains. He had asked an old timer about this, and was told if he held to the foothills he would be alright.

When he was past Colorado Springs, the country changed some. He was riding at the top of a bluff, and stopped to rest his horses. He walked over to the edge of the bluff and saw seven or eight wolves jumping toward a pockmark in the cliff. The pockmark was over five feet from the surface of the ground. The wolves apparently wanted what was in the pockmark.

Kelly went back and retrieved his Sharps that had a scope on it. He looked through the scope, and could tell a man was swinging a club at the wolves, as they attempted to jump onto the pockmark.

Kelly steadied his rifle on a rock that was about waist high, and took careful aim. His rifle made very little noise, but the shot went through one wolf, and into another, killing both.

He reloaded and shot again killing another wolf. He repeated this until only two wolves remained. They both then ran away, but Kelly took aim at the leader, and he fell. The other was now out of sight.

Kelly watched the person through his scope. He could now tell it was a woman. She climbed down from her perch and examined the dead wolves. She looked around in bewilderment. Kelly laughed at this, as the woman had not heard a thing, but the wolves were all dead. She then started walking toward Kelly, although some seventy to a hundred feet below him.

Kelly could see where an arroyo might give him a place to descend the cliff. It was very difficult, but after some time, he made it down to the surface, and rode toward the wolves. He could see the woman returning toward the wolves, so he waited.

Kelly said, "Why would you return, when you were nearly killed by those wolves?"

The woman, who appeared to be a half breed, said in perfect English, "For the pelts of course. They are worth a dollar a piece." She then knelt, and began skinning the wolves with a sharp skinning knife. Kelly got down, and began helping her.

As they worked the woman asked, "How did you shoot those wolves without your rifle making any noise?"

"I have a devise that keeps it silent. It is very useful when hunting."

"When we are finished with the wolves, I will feed you, and put you up for the night."

It was near dusk when they completed their task. Kelly loaded the pelts onto his horse and they left. They had walked about a quarter of a mile, when they came to an opening in the cliff. It was about twenty-five to thirty feet across, but had been closed by an adobe wall that went up some ten to twelve feet. There was a door, but it had been painted the same color as the adobe, and the adobe was the same color as the cliff, making it practically invisible.

The woman said, "Take your horse through the door, and on through to the back door, which Kelly did. When he was out back, he could tell that the woman had closed in a box canyon that only went back about a hundred feet. As it was getting dark, Kelly unsaddled his horse, and rubbed him down with a towel he kept in his saddle bag. The woman gave his horse some corn, and dragged a tub of water over for him. When the horse was taken care of, they returned to the adobe house. It was neat as a pin, and a fire was burning in a stone fireplace.

The woman, who looked to be in her late thirties or early forties, was fixing something on the hearth. She said, "My husband and I found this place when we were hunting. I had been raised by the Hopi Indians, and knew how to make adobe and build with it. We decided to wall in the canyon, and make it our home. My husband was a skilled carpenter. He built the fireplace, and covered the walls and ceiling with wood so we would not have so much dust. The floor is slate, as is the roof. He put a pipe under the house to take out the access water from the spring out back. It flows year-round, and never freezes, as he put the water pipe underground. He put in a cistern with a pump, so I always have fresh water here in the house. The spring waters our garden and trees. It is an ideal place to live."

"Where is your husband?"

"He died last year of the miseries. I buried him out back."

"You speak perfect English. Tell me how you came to learn that."

"My mother was a Hopi Indian. My father was a white soldier. He came though that part of New Mexico and bought her from her father.

"My parents died and I was placed in a school run by some missionaries, and was educated. When I was about seventeen, a young man came by and was taken in by the missionaries. He had been wounded in a fight with a hostile Ute. It took about six months before he was healed. I was assigned to feed him, and take care of his needs. We became enamored with one another and married. We never had children although we wanted them.

"My husband was offered a job with a lumber company, so we moved to Pueblo. He worked as a carpenter after his job with the lumber company petered out. We did alright, but didn't like Pueblo. My husband liked to hunt, and I always went with him. On one of our trips, we found this place, and both fell in love with it. We lived here over ten years before he died. It was a happy ten years. Now I'm alone. I think I would like some children, now. I will pay you fifty dollars a piece for a boy and a girl. I want them under four, so I can raise them in the ways of my Lord, Jesus. Would you do that for me?"

"I don't know why not. There are always orphan children looking for a home. I'll see what I can do when I reach Pueblo."

"Tell them that Mr. and Mrs. Brian Hunt desires to give the children a home. Most people knew us, and knew that we were good 'church-goin' people, and that I have a nice home for the children to live in."

"I will tell them, Mrs. Hunt."

"Just call me Olga. What's your name?"

"I'm Kelly Andrews."

"What do you do for a living, Mr. Andrews?"

"I'm a gambler, Olga. I will secure the children before I disclose my profession, though."

When Kelly reached Pueblo, he rented a room at the hotel. It had a dining room and a bar. He stayed away from the bar, and had dinner that night at the hotel. Before he ate he inquired about a church. There was a Catholic Church that had an early service and a protestant church that had a service at eleven. He had no luck at the Catholic church, but at the protestant church he was informed that there were twins, who were three years old, being kept at Mrs. Talbot's boarding house.

Kelly had worn his suit and tie and called on Mrs. Talbot. She remembered the Hunts and thought they would make great parents. She actually wanted rid of the twins, as she wasn't paid anything to keep them.

Kelly rented a buggy, and with the twins and their belongings, took them out to Olga's home. She met them with a smile, and immediately gave them some cake that she had baked. The children were not treated well at Mrs. Talbot's home, and were glad to be with someone else.

Olga tried to pay him a hundred dollars, but Kelly refused and said, "I want the hundred dollars to go to the children. Kelly then told Olga that he just had the buggy for the day, and returned before dark. He decided to go to a saloon, that he knew had gambling. He didn't play at first. He watched from the bar. None of the men were professionals, and that was obvious to Kelly. He watched a large man, who seemed to be winning. He asked a saloon girl who the big winner was.

She said, That's Bob Burns, the owner of the B bar B ranch. He owns that and everything else in Pueblo. Don't ever cross him, or you will be sorry."

"Has he punished anyone lately?"

"Yes, about four week ago he was playing cards with a young Mexican cowboy. The cowboy took a large sum of money from Burns. Burns accused him of cheating, and had him arrested. However, there has been no trial, so the cowboy just rots in jail.

"You see those two cowboys, who are watching the poker game?"

Kelly nodded and she said, "Those are Burns' men. They are actually his bodyguards. Don't fool with them, they are vicious. I saw them beat a man so badly that he was in bed for a week."

"Didn't the law do anything about it?"

"The law! Good luck there, Burns owns the law. The man who was beaten was arrested for assault. Of course there was no trial. They let him out a month later and told him to leave Pueblo"

Kelly could see that she was a wealth of information and said, "I like you. What's your name?"

"I'm Rosa Amour, but it is not my real name."

"My name is Kelly and I like your name."

"Are you looking for a little sport, Kelly?"

"I may be. I'll give you fifty cents if you will help me out with a little joke."

"What do I have to do?"

"I want you to walk toward those two bodyguards. I will pass you on my way out the back to relieve myself. I'll swat you on the rump. You then push me towards those guards."

"Please don't confront those men, Kelly, they will beat you half to death."

"I won't, just do what I say," and he handed her a fifty cent piece. She started toward the men and Kelly passed her, and swatted her on the rump. She laughed and pushed him toward the men. Kelly fell onto them and said, "I'm sorry. It looks like I'm falling for Rosa."

Both men laughed and one said, "You need to get some spectacles, man."

Kelly looked back at her and said, "I like her." He then went out the back, as Rosa asked the guards if they wanted another round.

When Kelly returned one of the guards said, "I haven't seen you before. What are you doing in Pueblo?"

"Just passing through." He then looked at the other guard and said, "Did you know your partner has your wallet and watch? The man was shocked, and immediately felt for his wallet and watch. Not finding them, He turned to his partner and said, "Is this a joke?"

His partner said, "I didn't take them," but this didn't stop his partner, as he put his hand into his partner's coat pocket. That produced the wallet and watch. A fight ensued. The one who was robbed, shot the other dead.

A hush came over the room and someone said, "Get the sheriff." The sheriff arrived and the matter was discussed. It was finally decided that it was self defense. Kelly then spoke up and said, "Sheriff, the dead man's gun is still in its holster?"

The sheriff then said, "He's right. Hank never drew his gun. I'll have to arrest you Dude." Burns then stood and said, "Now wait up there, Herb. I said it was self defense, and that's what it'll be." The sheriff didn't want to accept that, but swallowed hard and said, "Whatever you say, Mr. Burns."

Burns then looked at Kelly and said, "Who asked your opinion?"

"It wasn't an opinion, it was merely an observation. I don't want to be involved, as I am just passing through."

"Well, you are involved, because you questioned me."

"No Sir, I did not question you, I just said that the man still had his gun in its holster. That is merely an observation that I thought the sheriff would be interested in."

"Lock him up for the night, Herb, and fine him the amount of cash that he has in his wallet."

The sheriff said, "Give me your gun."

"I'm not wearing one." Kelly turned to Rosa and said, "Would you store my things in your room, Rosa?"

Shé smiled and said, "Sure, Big Boy. "She then looked at the sheriff and said, "Leave a couple of dollars in his wallet, Sheriff, he will need some comforting when you let him out tomorrow," and everyone laughed.

Actually Kelly had most of his money in his hidden pocket under his saddle. He had hoped that he would be jailed, so that he may have a chance to talk to Valdez. He was put in the cell next to Valdez. There was no one else in the jail and they were locked away from the office.

Kelly waited until it was quiet. He then said, "Lenard Valdez."

"How do you know my name?"

"I was sent to see what happened to you. When the postcards quit coming, I was sent to see why."

"That Burns has an iron hand on this town. I might be here forever. I beat him out of some money, and he is a sore loser, so he accused me of cheating. There was nothing I could do, as two of his henchmen said they saw me cheating."

Kelly said, "Burns told the sheriff to just hold me overnight and to fine me the amount of money I had in my wallet. I only had ten dollars in it, so they won't get much. By the way, the reason I'm in here is that one of Burns' guards shot the other. They called it self defense. I pointed out that the one who was shot, still had his gun in its holster. That made Burns mad, so he ordered the sheriff to put me in jail, and confiscate all my money.

"By the way, don't you have the derringer in your boot?"

"Yeah, I thought of that. But if I brought it out, and have no horse nor money, what would I do. If I were to steal a horse, they would hang me for sure. So I just bided my time. I knew Colonel Alfred would send someone. How are you going to get me out of here?"

"I think the bigger question is how are we going to bring Burns to justice."

"The justice for him is at the end of a rope, or some lead in his belly."

"Now don't get sore, a mad agent is not worth anything, because he makes mistakes. I'll figure out something tomorrow. Let's get some sleep."

CHAPTER 5

BRINGING DOWN BURNS

The next morning the sheriff came early, and let Kelly out. The sheriff said, "I'm letting you out before breakfast. That way, we don't have to feed you."

Kelly went to the saloon where Rosa worked. The door was not locked, but the barkeep said, "We're closed."

"I'm here to see Rosa."

"Upstairs. Her room is the first one on the right."

"Kelly went up and knocked on the door. Rosa shouted, "Leave me alone."

"Kelly said, "Mr. Burns wants to see you."

Rosa jumped out of bed, and began putting on a robe. She said in a scared voice, "What does he want with me?"

"He's thinking about arresting you for helping that cowboy, who was jailed last night."

As she was unlocking her door she said, "I was just being a good neighbor." She then opened the door. She said, "I ought to brain you, Kelly, you scared me half out of my wits."

Kelly said, "Get dressed, and I'll buy you a good breakfast."

"Well, you ought to, you scared me terribly."

"Come on in while I dress." Rose had a room screen that she dressed behind. While she was doing this, Kelly retrieved twenty dollars from the hidden pocket inside his saddle."

While Rose was dressing she said, "You ought to buy me lunch also, as that saddle of yours weighs a ton, and I had to cart it, and all your other things over here. I had to make two trips."

"I really appreciate what you did for me, Rosa. I guess this makes us friends for good."

"I don't know how much good there is in it. I hoped to get real friendly with you tonight. By the way, how are you going to buy my breakfast. Burns told the sheriff to fine you all your money."

"I never carry but a few dollars in my wallet. Too many bad guys. I hid some of my money, so I will have enough for breakfast, lunch and a little fun on the side."

They were now in a café that Rose knew, and were eating. Kelly said, "How would you like to be employed by me? I would give you three dollars a week."

"That's only three pokes. Are you trying to bargain?"

"I'm not paying for pokes. I just want you to be my partner. I need a lot of information, and have no way of getting it without stirring up some of Burns' friends. He pays off so many people, I don't know who they might be."

"Well, I'm surely not one of his fans. He called me old, once. Maybe I'm a bit older than the other girls. It made me feel real bad."

"Well, you may be older than the other girls, but you are much prettier, and I like women who are out of the giggling stage."

"You say all the right things a girl wants to hear, Kelly. Sure, I'll be your partner. What are you trying to know?"

"For one, do you think I should play cards with Burns?"

"Not if you take a lot of money from him. Let him win some, then take his money slowly if you are good enough. Burns is pretty good at cards."

"No, he thinks he's good at cards, because he can beat the locals. He's just an amateur. He needs someone to give him a real good lesson."

"If you give it to him, he will have you jailed forever."

"Well, I guess we will just have to see."

Rosa said, "Don't say I didn't warn you. I had better keep your saddle and things in my room, as I don't want to tote them again. I'd let you stay with me, but we're not allowed to have men stay over night."

Kelly winked at her and said, "That's alright, I'll get more sleep at the hotel."

Rosa laughed and said, "You may be good, but you're not that good. I'd ride you down like a sick horse."

"Is that a challenge?"

"No, a promise," and they both laughed.

They had finished their breakfast and Kelly said, "Is there a park here or someplace we could talk. I would like to know more about you."

"I'd like that. We have a nice park that isn't that far. I need to get more exercise."

They reached the park and Kelly said, "Now tell me your life's story."

"I was married when I was eighteen to a bank clerk here. We lived a good life, and went to church every Sunday. I enjoyed life then. We had two children, both girls. Both were in their teens when Teddy was caught embezzling from the bank. He swore he didn't do it, but couldn't prove it. They gave him twenty years. He died in prison a few years ago. The girls were in their teens. They took them away from me, and sent them to the state orphanage in Denver. I don't know where they are now, they never came back.

I tried to get a job clerking or working as a maid. No one would hire me. I asked why, and was told that they couldn't trust me. There was nothing left to do, but be a sporting woman or kill myself. I chose to be a sporting woman.

"I liked a man's love and Teddy was a good lover. So, I came to this saloon, and Sam hired me. He said he was sorry, but that the life here wasn't so bad. I was really glad to get the job. It's not so bad. I don't have any friends, but those giggling girls. But they're alright. Now I have you. You can't believe how much I value your friendship. All the other men treat me like the whore I am, but you never did. Now tell me about yourself."

"Pretty boring if you ask me. When I was eighteen, I was put into uniform, and fought for the South. I killed many men, and a few boys during the war. I tried to just look at them as objects that had to be killed to win the war. I was in the cavalry. I learned to ride quite well and along the way, I was taught about playing cards. A master of cards taught me. He could take a deck of card, shuffle it three times, and have you cut the cards. He could then deal you anything in the world. I could never match him, but I did learn a lot. The best thing I learned from him, is how to read men when they play. I can nearly tell you what they have in their hands when I play. Betting is one of the nuances that has to be learned. Bet too much, and the others will fold. Bet too little, and you don't make much on good hands. The good players know when and how much to bet. Poker is more skill than luck. Watch me tonight.

"After the war, I wanted to be away from every human on earth. I took a job as a cowboy near Springfield, Missouri. I was by myself most of the time. I enjoyed the solitude, and mainly not having to kill anyone. I still have nightmares like so many men, who went to war. I think my attitude about not looking at the men I killed as humans helped, or maybe I am so much of a killer it doesn't bother me. You are about the only friend I have. I met a girl along the way, and was very close to her one night. We didn't make love, but we both knew we loved each other. I got a job with a company in Topeka, and had to leave her. She said she would wait for me, but that was over a year ago, I'm sure she didn't. She had men hanging round her like honeybees to a hive.

"I went back to gambling. It's a good living, and I do my best not to take money from those who can't afford to lose.

"Watch me tonight, you will probably be amazed."

That night about nine o'clock Kelly arrived at the saloon. He was dressed nicely, but was not overdressed. He had a drink and watched the card game.

Burns was playing and said, "I see you have some money again. Do you want to chance some of it?"

"That depends, Mr. Burns. Will you have me locked up if I win some money from you?"

"Not if you don't cheat."

"I don't cheat, as I never deal the cards. I let others deal, so there is no way to cheat. I like to cut the cards, though. I like to feel the deck, so I know that all the card are there."

"No one can do that," Burns said.

"Would you like to wager on it, Mr. Burns?"

"Yes. I will get three brand new decks, and have someone take a card or two from two of the decks. Then you can feel them, and tell me which is a full deck."

"Good enough. A full deck has fifty-three cards with the joker. I will tell you how many cards are in each of the three decks."

"It's a bet," Burns said. He then said, "How about fifty dollars?"

"That will be okay. Fifty on each deck. But before we start, you must say fifty on each deck."

"This irritated Burns, but he said, "Fifty dollars on each deck, but I want to see your money." Kelly laid down three fifty dollar bills. Burns took the decks and turned his back to Kelly while he took some cards, and inserted others in the decks.

The three decks were then placed in front of Kelly. He picked up the first deck and felt it. He then sat it down and said, "That deck has fifty three card in it."

The cards were counted and fifty three were counted. Kelly then picked up the second deck and felt it. He sat just a second or two and said, "That deck has fifty-five cards in it."

The deck was counted and fifty-five was in it. Kelly then picked up the third deck, and sat it down quickly and said that deck has fifty-one." The deck was counted and fifty-one was the number."

Burns brought out his wallet and said, "Incredible. I would have paid a hundred and fifty to see that. Do you play poker?"

"Yes, but I never deal. That way, no one can say I cheated. I only touch the cards that I play. I do, however, feel the deck before it is dealt."

Burns said, "Fair enough. We will get a dealer, who doesn't play, so that it's fair to everyone. He said, "Bart, you are pretty good at dealing. You deal."

There were five in the game. There wasn't many good hands for awhile. Then there was a deal where Burns upped the ante by ten dollars. Very few times anyone even raised two dollars. Kelly studied Burns for awhile then said, "I see your ten and twenty more." Burns had thought he could buy the pot, and was furious, so he folded.

The very next hand Kelly called Burns after several raises. He laid down three deuces and Burns threw his cards at the wall. The game then began to heat up. Burns was now betting heavily, so Kelly just laid back, and picked him clean when he had a good hand. Finally Burns said, "That's all for me tonight, but *card-man* don't you leave town. I'll want my money back tomorrow night."

Kelly said, "Why don't you let the man out you said was a card cheat, and I will tell you whether he's a cheat or just a good card player?"

Burns thought about this and said, "Where would he get any money to play?"

"When I was in jail with him, he told me that he had money in the Denver bank, and could write a check if they ever let him out."

Burns said, "I'll think about it."

After Burns left, Rosa came over and said, "How much did you take off of Burns and the others?"

"A hundred dollars and some change, plus the hundred and fifty on the decks.."

"You had better stay with me tonight."

"I thought you said Sam didn't allow men to stay overnight."

"He doesn't, but he might make an exception as he saw you take Burns for a bundle, and will think what I'm thinking."

"And what's that?"

"Someone will be in your hotel room tonight."

Rosa talked to Sam and he said, "I'll give him Elle's room. She's out of town visiting some kin."

The next day Kelly went to his room. It had been trashed by someone who was looking for his money. Kelly didn't have anything in the room, but everything was turned over and the mattress even split. Kelly called the hotel manager and he said, "I should have known. I heard how you fleeced Burns last night. If I were you, Sonny, I would get my horse and travel."

"Burns told me not to leave town, so I know I'm being watched."

The hotel manager said, "I wouldn't exchange places with you, even if you were a millionaire. Burns can't stand to lose."

"Well, then someone should take him down a peg or two."

"So many people get money from him, that they would turn in their own mother, if it brought them more of his money."

The next day, Lenard Valdez came into the saloon about mid-afternoon. He asked Kelly to go to the bank with him. Kelly did that, and Valdez wrote a check for two hundred dollars.

They rested that afternoon and talked about the coming game. They decided to play the old game of partners. Kelly was sure Burns had a partner, because he had seen them signal one another. It was just funny to Kelly, as they both were left with mud on their face many times. He even saw Burns glare at his partner a time or two when the hands went against them.

Lenard and Kelly were much more subtle with their signals, as they had been trained by the best. The game started at around eight. There was now a crowd around them. In just the second hand, Lenard took twemty dollars from Burns. Burns knew he didn't cheat as a dealer was used that was not in the game. Burns' partner was a merchant. A doctor was another player, then Lenard and Kelly.

Not an hour into the game the doctor had dropped out as he could see that Burns was becoming angry On a hand that Burns thought he couldn't lose, as he had a flush, Lenard had a full house. That cost Burns nearly a fifty dollars, as Kelly stayed in the game until nearly the last, as did Burns' partner.

Burns was so angry that he drew his pistol and shot Lenard. Kelly had anticipated this, and as he turned his gun toward Kelly, Kelly shot him through the head with his derringer.

Someone sent for the sheriff. No one left the saloon. When the sheriff arrived he was told by several witness, that Burns had drawn his gun and shot Valdez. He was about to shoot Kelly, when Kelly shot him dead with his derringer. The sheriff could see that he couldn't do anything, so he asked Kelly and a couple of witness to come to his office to write out a statement. Valdez was taken to the doctors house. He extracted the bullet and told everyone that Valdez was out of danger.

However, one of Burns' men rode to the Burns' ranch, and told what happened. All were mad, as they knew their jobs would be gone, and the big paycheck that they received wouldn't be there anymore.

They next day, Burns' men rode to Pueblo to hang Valdez and Kelly. Sixteen men rode in. They went to the saloon to drink some courage. As they drank, their anger increased. Rosa came over to the doctor's office, and told Kelly that Burns' ranch hands were in town, and were coming to hang Lenard and he.

The doctor said, "I can hide Valdez in my basement. I have a special room down there. You will have to be on your own, Mr. Andrews. Kelly left immediately, and went to his hotel room. He went up the backstairs and retrieved his saddle and guns. He was saddled and gone within ten minutes.

A man came running into the bar and said, "I saw Andrews leaving town on his horse. All the Burns' crew left for their horses.

Kelly had purposely rode through town, so he could lead them away from the doctor's house. He could now see the dust behind him a mile or two. He rode to the area where he had descended the cliff. He dismounted and pulled his horse until they were on the top of the cliff looking down. He went to the same place where he had shot the wolves and dismounted. He tied his horse away, and got behind the rock.

He laid out a box of shells and had his rifle ready. As Burns' crew came into range, he started empting saddles. After the first three men fell, the others stopped. However, the empting of saddles didn't. They could not understand until one of the men said, "We are being shot at by a lot of men. It must be the army. I can't hear their rifles, but they are killing us. As he said these words, he fell from his saddle, his chest covered with blood. There were now just eight left. They all headed back for their ranch. Each packed his saddle bags with his gear, and was gone within ten minutes.

Kelly waited a few minutes, then rode back down the arroyo and picked up the bodies and dragged them over to the pockmark. He picked up the bodies and placed them in the pockmark.. It was now getting dark, so he went to Olga's house and knocked. She was very glad to see him. She had just cooked a stew and invited him to eat with her new family.

Kelly could see that the children really liked their new home and mother. When the children were in bed, Kelly told Olga what had happened. He told her he had placed eight bodies of his pursuers in the pockmark and asked if she would seal it up with adobe. He paid her a twenty dollars to do it. She said, "I really shouldn't take the money, as you have done so much for me, but the children will need the money."

Kelly said, "If you will go by the post office in June and December, you will find that I am sending them some money. Kelly kept his promise and sent a fifty dollars in June and December.

The next morning early, he rode back to Pueblo. He stopped by the doctor's office and told him that the Burns' gang was no more.

The doctor said, "How would you know that?"

"I just do. You will never see any of them again."

"Did you kill them all?"

"No, but they all left, as they knew they would be hanged if they stayed around."

Kelly went by the sheriff's office and said, "There is no one out at the Burns' ranch. The animals will be needing attention. The sheriff said, "I'll tend to it." The sheriff was thinking how he could get title to Burns' ranch.

The city council awarded Sam and Rosa the saloon as Burns owned it. They had to pay three hundred dollars for the transfer and a tax the council levied. They were given a year to pay it off. A year later, Sam married Rosa.

Kelly sent a letter to Washington DC telling the story of his time in Pueblo. He left out the part of killing half the Burns' gang. Olga went through the pockets of each man, and collected over three-hundred dollars, several watches and all their clothes. She reasoned that she could use the clothes to make clothes for her children. She then walled up the pock mark with the bodies in it.

CHAPTER 6

RETURN TO COFFEYVILLE

Kelly decided to use the railroad as much as possible. He had a free pass for him and his horse. He would end up in Omaha, but he could take a riverboat down the Missouri River to Kansas City, then ride to Coffeeville. It was a much longer trip, but very much shorter, time wise. Also, he would have no Indian trouble.

He was two days getting to Kansas City, and another two days riding to Coffeeville. He arrived at the La Barr ranch on a Saturday. No one seemed to be at home. He went to the barn where he found a Negro working.

Kelly said, "Are the La Barr's in town?"

The man had a wide grin on his face and said, "Yes Sir, Ms. Patty is getting married today. You had better ride fast or you'll miss the ceremony."

Kelly rode to Coffeeville as fast as he could without killing his horse. He could see a large gathering at the church, and ran his horse there. He entered the door just as the minister asked, "Does anyone have a reason why this couple should not be wed?"

Kelly, in a loud voice said, "Yes, Harold and I do."

Everyone was shocked and turned to see a man, who had dust from one end of him to the another. His face was covered with dust, so that his

52

teeth seemed shinny and his eyes bright. The minister said, "And what is your objection, Sir?"

"Because I want to save this gentleman from a bad marriage."

"Why would the marriage be bad, Sir?"

"Because she loves Harold and me, and only us."

The crowd made a great noise, as they took in their breath. Richard Thomas, her fiancé, said, "How the hell did you get that idea?"

"Because she told us she did. I have been gone for over a year, and could not write. She didn't know this, or she would never have agreed to marry you. As I said, she loves only Harold an me."

"Who the hell is Harold?"

"Harold has a strong attachment to me, and goes where I go. He is like a wet noodle most of the time, but I can assure you, when I need him, he can rise up and be counted."

"Do you know this man and Harold, Patty?"

"Yes, I know him and Harold, and I love them both. Harold brought us close together. I can vouch for him. He laid his head against me one night and I have loved him ever since. I can assure you he can stand tall when needed."

No one got the significance of what they were saying about Harold, but then it hit La Barr, He began laughing so hard he shook. He went to his knees, as he was laughing so hard he couldn't stand. Someone said, "You had better look at Leland, doctor, he is having a seizure or maybe a stroke.

As the doctor started forward, Richard Thomas turned to Patty and said, "I'm glad I found out what nuts you and your family are before I got tied up with you. He shoved her away, and started down the aisle in a hurry. When he got to Kelly, he swung at him with a haymaker. Kelly had anticipated this and ducked. Thomas' blow hit his aunt on the jaw and knocked her cold. He then realized what he had done, and began tending to his aunt. Patty came flying down the aisle and Kelly met her halfway. They kissed. Dirt was now all over her white dress and her face, but she didn't seem to mind at all.

By this time La Barr had recovered, and came forward to where the couple stood and said, "I will never again find anything as funny as you two. He then began to laugh again.

Patty said, "Daddy now knows Harold. If nothing else, he got the laugh of his life."

The three of them left for Leland's ranch. He drove the buggy. Kelly and Patty rode in the second seat, with Kelly's horse tied to the back. Every once in awhile La Barr would shake his head and laugh again. He said, "You two were met for each other. Thomas was a fine man, but was never in you and Harold's league," and with that went into a spasm of laughter. He then said, "It's the best joke in the world, and I can't share it with anyone."

Patty said, "You had better not, Daddy, or I will skin you alive."

Patty drew Kelly a bath and La Barr brought him a drink while he was in the tub. Leland said, "Patty come in here. I can't wait to hear Kelly's story. There is just the four of us and you know Harold." With that La Barr went in to a fit of laughter.

Kelly said, "You can never repeat anything I tell you as it is a national secret." This brought them to lean forward.

Kelly told in detail how he now worked for the Federal Government in a secret organization. He said, "The training lasted a full year, and we were not allowed to communicate with anyone. Then just as I finished the training, I was sent to Colorado to rescue another agent. He had gotten himself jailed in the town of Pueblo. That took another two months." He told them about Burns, but did not tell them about him killing Burns and half his crew.

"I did send you that postcard. Did you get it?"

"Yes, but you just said you were on an assignment and would write when you could." I was then going with Richard. He's a fine man, who has a future in his father's business. I thought you would never come back. When Richard asked me to marry him, I decided this would be the best bet I would ever have, so I agreed to marry him. Daddy told me not to, but said, I must follow my own feelings. Daddy likes you nearly as much as I do. I saw that right away."

Kelly was now clean and he asked for a towel. Patty fetched one and said, "I had better start dinner," and left.

La Barr said, "You cut it a might thin, Kelly. What would you have done if you had been a half hour later?"

"I thought of that on my ride in, as your man told me about the wedding. I decided I would just go get her wherever she was. She loves me and I love her. I have to go to Washington DC. My employment is there. I need to hand in my resignation. I intend to take Patty with me. I would like to get married before we leave.

"As I caused such a stir in town, I thought I would take Patty to town, and get a marriage license. We can then go by the preacher's house, and have him marry us in his house. His wife and you can witness it."

"Have you told Patty your plans?"

"No, I haven't had time to think this through. Do you have any objections?"

"No, but I do have some questions. How are you going to support her?"

"I haven't got that far yet. I have a lot of skills now, and I know I can make a living about anywhere?"

"Doing what?"

"I'm a fair gambler. I was taught by the best. I never deal the cards, so I could never be accused of cheating. I can read the faces of the men I gamble with. The cards really have very little to do with winning. After I have played with a man a few hands, I can tell some, by his betting. Nearly everyone has things about them, that give away their hands. As I said, "I was taught by the best."

"Well, you may be the best in the world, but there are sore losers that can't stand to be beat. They may kill you. I've heard there are others who play as a team, and they are hard to beat."

"Actually they are easier to beat. It takes only an hour or two to recognize this activity, then I use it to my advantage. I can recognize nearly every manner of cheating while they are dealing. I can recognize marked decks. I was playing with a man in Pueblo who brought in a marked deck. I used it to my advantage. When the man dealt, I would pick up my cards while he was dealing, so he couldn't see my cards. I could read his and the others. I have been taught to see, and remember cards. It is now second nature to me. I took a lot of money from him, then exposed his marked deck to the other players."

"Well, you may be good, but that kind of livin' generally leads to not livin'. I hope you have something else lined up. Your children won't like it when they are asked, 'What does your father do for a livin'?'"

"Oh, I plan to look around and an opportunity will come up, it always does."

At supper that night, Kelly asked Patty if she would like to go to Washington DC on their honeymoon. She was thrilled and said, "When are we going to be married?"

"Tomorrow is a good day."

La Barr drove them in, and they got their license and the minister married them. La Barr had tied his horse to the back of the buggy before leaving, and told Kelly that the buggy and horse were his wedding present to them. They said their goodbyes and Patty promised her father she would write along the way.

The trip to Kansas City was nice, as they were in love. Kelly told her about his involvement with the government, and that she could never say anything about it, as it was top secret.

They caught the train at Kansas City and had many stops and changes of railroads along the way. Kelly told Patty that he wanted to take her to New Orleans via a ship, then up the Mississippi, to see the many sights along the way. Kelly knew there would be many card games on the riverboats.

In Washington, Kelly met with Colonel Alfred. Alfred congratulated Kelly and said, "Valdez has already been here, and is gone on another assignment. We only have a few men as agents."

"How many?" Kelly asked.

Alfred said, "Six at present. We have many who drop out, as it is a stressful job and many men can't take it."

Kelly said, "I don't want to drop out, but I would like a long rest. Is that okay?"

"Yes. We don't have anything going at this time that would fit you. I would like you to write us a card each week, and tell where you will be the next week. Is that okay?"

"I'll do my best to keep you informed, but I plan to move about seeing America."

They left for New York City, as both wanted to see it. They stayed four days, and made reservations on a ship that would take them to New Orleans.

Aboard the ship there were poker games. Kelly watched the table where the highest stakes were played. There was always a crowd that watched this table. Kelly picked out the sharp players immediately, and watched how they bet and their mannerisms. The two sharpest players expressions never changed. They were conservative players, and patiently waited for the cards to come to them. He did notice one had a habit of tapping his left forefinger once in awhile. It was a very small thing, but each time he had a winning hand, he would tap it on the table every so lightly. When his hand was only mediocre the tapping never occurred.

Patty wanted to go to bed, and Kelly asked if it were alright if he watched some more, and she encouraged him to stay. After two men dropped out, Kelly asked if he could sit in. He laid down two hundred dollars in bills and change. It was table stakes so you could only bet what was in front of you.

Kelly noticed that the other sharp player seemed to have better hands when the person tapping his finger was dealing and vice-versa. This told him that the tapping was a signal, and that they were dealing each other good hands. He then picked up on the other partner touching his eyebrow when he had a good hand. Both players were now far ahead.

Kelly was dealt a fair hand of two pair, with aces over. This told Kelly they were setting him up. He recognized a second card deal when they were asked for cards. He received a card that gave him a full house. The partner of the *tapper* made a big bet and the *tapper* just called. Kelly folded and saw a surprised look on the dealers face. Kelly then said, "I guess it is just not my night." However, Kelly had palmed the two aces.

When it became the *tapper's* deal he was again dealt two pair with aces over. Kelly asked for one card and was given another full house. He then switched the lower pair in his hand with the two aces he had palmed, and put the two cards in his hand onto some discarded cards near the pile of money when he bet. It was so smooth no one noticed. He now had four aces.

The *tapper* bet a large bet and Kelly raised him. He noticed a satisfied look on the partners face as he raised again. The *tapper* dropped out and Kelly pushed all his money into the middle and said, "I call."

The partner laid down four jacks. Kelly just sat there, and looked at the jacks without saying anything. When the partner went to rake in the money Kelly laid down the four aces. Everyone laughed, but the tapper and his partner.

The partner said, "I want to count the cards. This man obviously cheated."

"Count them," Kelly said.

The cards were counted then the partner turned all the cards over, and put them into suits. He could not believe what had happened.

Kelly said, "I guess I was just lucky."

The tapper glared at him and said, "I don't know how you did it, but you cheated."

Kelly said, "How would you like to cut the cards for everything that is in front of you, or are you too chicken?"

The tapper was now on the spot and knew it. He said, "Let me shuffle."

Kelly said, "No, and pointed to another man in the group who sat to Kelly's right and said, "Let him shuffle." The man shuffled and put the deck in front of Kelly. Kelly had nicked an ace ever so lightly. He felt the nick and cut the cards there. The *tapper* said, "I'll take the next card and the dealer turned it over. It was a king and the *tapper* smiled and said, "show us your cut. Kelly turned the deck up showing the ace. The *tapper* said, "You are either the luckiest man I ever met or the slickest cheat."

"That is the second time you called me a cheat. I find that losers always think they are cheated. Why can't you take it like a man instead of whimpering like some snotty nosed kid. I'm sure everyone here feels sorry for you. We'll let you have time to cry if you want."

The *tapper* was infuriated and reached for his vest pocket, but a man behind him grabbed his arm and said, "Let's throw this poor loser off the boat, and several men grabbed him.

Kelly never watched the *tapper*, because he was in good hands. However, he watched his partner and he was about to take some money from the man next to him during the melee, but Kelly reached across the table and grabbed his arm. The man whose money he was stealing said, "Let's throw both of them off the boat. Kelly calmly raked in all his money, and stayed out of the melee counting his money. He had won eight hundred dollars.

A man came back and said, "The captain stopped us, but he threw them in the brig. I guess that broke up the game."

It had all happened in an hour's time, and Kelly went to his room. Patty was reading and said, "How did the card game come out?"

"They caught two men cheating, and they were put in the ship's jail."

"I think those gamblers get what the deserve sooner or later."

"Yes, I'm sure they do."

CHAPTER 7

NEW ORLEANS

They were now in New Orleans, and saw the shows and all the places of interest. Patty said, "How can you afford all this?"

"I saved my money when I was a cowboy."

She laughed and said, "The government must pay you a great deal of money. Did you resign?"

"Not quite. I am on leave of absents. I thought I had better have something to fall back on. I can always quit if I don't like the next assignment."

Patty said, "You are a wily man. Did you pay those men to tie you up to me?"

"Of course, it was a set up all the way."

She laughed and said, "I wouldn't doubt it. You knew I had to know Harold."

"Absolutely! He's very close to me."

She pulled him to bed and said, "I need to know him better."

They caught a riverboat out of New Orleans, that was making numerous stops. Patty knew Kelly liked to watch the gambling, and she became interested. She said, "It seems to be a game of wits. Do you ever play?"

"Once in awhile, but sooner or later the gamblers lose, and I don't like to lose my hard earned cash."

"Hard earned? The most work I ever saw you do is ride from town to town. You always seem to be at the right place at the right time. I guess that is why the government employs you. What do you do for them?"

"I look into problems, and advise the government what should be done. It takes a lot of time to ferret out the solution to some problems."

"Is it ever dangerous?"

"Sometimes I get into a sticky situation, but I always say, 'safety first.'"

"You are very wise. I'm glad you don't carry a gun like so many of the men."

"Oh, I have them, but I keep them packed away. A man needs to have some protection, especially if he has a wife to look after."

They were now at Vicksburg. Kelly checked with the postmaster, but there were no messages. He then wrote a postcard saying he would be in Kansas City in a week or so. While he was doing that, Patty wrote her father about the marvelous trip they were taking, and how good Kelly was to her.

That night after dinner they again watched a poker game. Even Patty found it interesting to watch. There was a man dressed with a red velvet vest. His clothes were expensive, and he was wearing a diamond ring.

He seemed to win about every three hands, and had accumulated a lot of money. Patty said, "Do you suppose he's cheating?"

Kelly said, "No, he's just a superior player. He can read most of these men very easily. I can even see how stupid some of them play."

"Well, if you can see it, I suppose that dandy can read them like a book."

Patty said, "If you want to stay, it's okay. I want to read." She kissed his cheek and left. Two men withdrew about that time and Kelly asked, "Do you mind me sitting in?"

One said, "We need new money in this game."

Kelly sat down, and put two hundred dollars in front of him. He had watched everyone very closely for the past hour, and knew their habits pretty well. However, the dandy's expression never changed.

Kelly folded his first six hands without even asking for cards. He then drew four hearts, ace high. He asked for one and received another heart. The dandy hadn't dealt, so Kelly felt it okay to bet. The dandy bet five dollars, as it was his turn. The man to his left raised him five dollars. Two others folded, and Kelly just called the ten dollars. The rest folded in front of the dandy, but he raised again. This time twenty dollars, which was a very large bet. The man who raised before, folded his cards. Kelly studied his cards for a long time then raised the dandy twenty dollars. This shocked the dandy some, and after studying his cards some more folded.

Kelly said, "You were very wise my friend." He didn't show his cards, he just threw them in, and raked in the money. He folded the next seven times without taking cards. The dandy was now dealing and Kelly watched him carefully. He dealt from the bottom when giving Kelly cards. Kelly received three queens. Kelly studied the cards some, then just folded without asking for cards. He noted a surprised look, but it was subtle.

The very next deal Kelly received three fours. He only asked for one card. However, it was a four. The betting started, and the man to Kelly's right bet ten dollars. Kelly just called, but the man to the dandy's right raised five dollars. The dandy then raised twenty. The man to his left studied his cards, and just called. Kelly didn't study his cards, and raised a fifty. This shocked everyone. The dandy smiled and said, "Let's make it a hundred. The man to the dandies left said, "That's too rich for my blood," and folded.

Kelly said, "Let's make it interesting," and put the rest of his money into the pot, which totaled just over two hundred and fifty dollars. This made the daddy think. He had too much in the pot to fold so he called him. Kelly laid down the four fours, and the dandy threw his cards on the table face down.

Kelly was raking the money. The man next to the dandy said, "You only took one card. I figured you for a straight or a flush. Had you been dealing, I would have questioned your integrity," and everyone laughed, but the dandy. He was fuming. Most of his money was gone, so he handed the attendant some large bills to break down. When the attendant returned, Kelly could see the money amounted to five hundred dollars.

They played several more hands and Kelly folded all without asking for cards. The dandy played nearly every hand, and was winning most of them. Then the man to Kelly's left was dealing. He was not the swiftest of players, but Kelly watched him closely anyway. He could detect no improprieties with his dealing. Kelly picked up his cards, and had four low clubs. It only lacked the five to be a straight flush. The dandy took two cards. Another took one, and Kelly asked for one. It was the five of clubs.

The betting started and was quite lively. Kelly just called each time, but the dandy raised each time. The last time it was a fifty dollar raise. All dropped out, but Kelly. He studied his cards for a long time then said, "I'll raise a hundred."

The dandy smiled and said, "Let's make it interesting and pushed all his money forward. The attendant counted the money of the dandy and said, "It comes to six hundred and forty-two dollars."

Kelly counted out the same amount from his pile of money and pushed them forward and said, "What do you have?" The dandy laid down four nines with an evil smile.

Kelly didn't change expressions, he just sat there a moment. The dandy started to rake the money when Kelly laid down his straight flush." There were gasps.

The dandy was incensed. He said, I have five hundred dollars in my wallet. Will you cut the cards for five hundred?"

Kelly said, "Why not."

The dandy started to pick up the cards, but Kelly said, "Let someone else shuffle the cards," so the dandy put down the cards. It was the man to Kelly's right who picked up the cards and shuffled them. He then put down the deck in front of Kelly. Kelly ran his hands over the edge of the cards and felt a slight nick on one of them. He cut the cards at that point, and just held it waiting for the dandy to draw. The dandy ran his hand over the edge of the deck looking for the nick. Kelly said, "I already have the card you are looking for, as it had a nick in it," and turned over an ace.

The dandy put his hand in his breast pocket, brought out a derringer and pointed at Kelly. The man just to the dandy's right said, "You pull that trigger, and we'll tie your hands and feet together, and throw you overboard. We're going to throw you overboard anyway, but you will have a fighting chance to swim to shore if you put that gun away. The dandy complied, and the men marched him outside. They stripped him, and threw him overboard naked.

The captain arrived and said, "What happened?"

One of the man said, "This guy was losing at the card table, and all of a sudden he came out here and began taking his clothes off. He then jumped in naked. None of us knew what he was doing until he jumped."

The captain said, "It happens every now and then," and returned to the helm.

Kelly had not gone outside. He was counting his money and exchanging the coins for folding money. He was told what happened, when one of the women ran in and was telling another attendant what had happened.

Kelly returned to his room and Patty was still reading. She looked up and said, "Was it interesting?"

"More than you can imagine. They caught the dandy cheating, stripped him, and threw him overboard. He will make it to shore, but will have a hard time explaining why he's naked."

"Serves him right. It just shows you, that gamblers never win. In the end they all get what's due them."

"And what's that, Patty?"

"I don't know, I was just gabbing away," and both laughed.

"Kelly didn't play anymore the rest of the trip. He was asked by several to join the table, but Kelly refused. Patty said, "He's not much of a poker player," and all the men laughed. This puzzled her, and she turned to Kelly and said, "Did I say anything funny?"

Kelly said, "It was just their way of saying, 'You're right,' without embarrassing me."

In Kansas City, Kelly had given Patty a hundred dollars. He told her to go buy herself some clothes. He said, "Please don't make me go with you."

She laughed and said, "It will be more fun without looking at your pained face."

Kelly went straight to the post office. There was a thick letter from Colonel Alfred. It told Kelly that he was needed to locate another agent who had disappeared. The agent had been investigating a gang who was shaking down the citizens of Chicago. The man's name was Clark Smith. He quit sending in his post cards two weeks ago.

The letter went on to say the boss of the gang was a Mr. William "Bill" Buchanan. It was estimated that Bill had over twenty men on his payroll, and none of them had any means of support except from Bill Buchanan.

The letter said, "That if you accept this mission, you will be paid a lump sum of two thousand dollars. You must also bring down Bill

Buchanan and his game. The two thousand will include your expenses, also."

Kelly thought about it and thought, *"I wonder how long the job will take. It will take me sometime to infiltrate Buchanan's gang and get the information. Clark Smith is likely dead, but I would have to have proof of that."*

Kelly met Patty at the hotel for lunch. He just handed her the letter. She read it and said, "Can you do this?"

"Yes, but it will take me some time."

"How much time?"

"Probably six months, but it could be much less."

"How dangerous is it?"

"I really don't know, but I think I can handle it. Bringing down a gang isn't that hard. You must first get the members to fight among themselves. They will kill each other. After that, the survivors will probably move, as they will be wanted by the police."

"Two thousand dollars is a lot of money. What would be your plans if you are successful?"

"I was thinking of being a landlord in California. If we could buy a hotel, it could be quite lucrative."

"A hotel. That would be much more expensive than two thousand dollars."

"I know, but I'm always able to pick up a lot of money when I take down a gang as big as this."

"Have you done this before?"

"Yes. When I was gone the last time. How do you think I was able to pay for that expensive trip to New York and New Orleans?"

"I'm so simple, I didn't even think about it. I just knew you knew what you were doing."

"Well, you still haven't answered my question. Will you be alright living with your father for a few months?"

"Of course. He expects me back, and told me so. He loves to have me there. He's so fun to be around, that I look forward to it."

"Then it's settled. I'll go on to Chicago, and you will go back to Coffeyville. Here's a thousand dollars. You may want to buy your dad a thing or two."

CHAPTER 8

CHICAGO

When Kelly arrived in Chicago, he went to a clothier, and obtained a new wardrobe. He stored his old clothes with the clothier. He now had two suits, a frock coat, a derby hat, a top hat and new shoes.

He made some inquiries about Bill Buchanan. He found out where he did his drinking, where he dined, what activities he liked and if he had a family or just girlfriends.

He started with the Belvedere. It was an upscale tavern. The drinks were more expensive to keep the rabble out. Kelly entered the place, and went to the bar. There were only a few men at the bar, as it was only seven in the evening. He ordered a whiskey, then turned his back to the bar to survey the crowd. There were several woman who worked the crowd. Kelly made eye contact with one.

She immediately came over and said, "Would you like to take a table, and buy me a drink?"

Kelly said, "Why not." She ordered, and the bartender poured her a drink. She then led the way to a table against the far wall, where no one was sitting.

She asked, "Are you new in town?"

"Yes, and I would like to know something about Chicago, so I don't learn the hard way."

"Why, we're a quiet town. Bill Buchanan sees to that."

"Who's Bill Buchanan?"

"The man who controls everything that happens in Chicago."

"Is he the mayor?"

"No, but he controls the mayor, chief of police and all the councilmen. Nothing gets done without his say so."

"My, he is a powerful man."

"The reason I'm telling you this, is to keep you from getting into trouble. Please don't tell anyone that I told you this."

"Well, I will tell you some things that I hope you will keep under your hat."

"And what is that?"

"I'm here to find a friend of mine who just seemed to disappear."

"Oh," the woman said, "That happens when someone gets crosswise with Buchanan. That is the reason I told you about Buchanan. Who is your friend?"

"Clark Smith, but he could have been using an alias."

"I haven't heard the name. By the way, my name is Lola. It's not my real name, but I don't want people knowing that. I came to work here when my husband had an accident, and couldn't hold a job. I have no skills, so the only thing for me was working as a saloon girl. I don't have to bed men, as the manager does not allow that activity. That is the only reason I work here. If you are looking for sport, you won't find it here. I'm sure some of the girls have a sideline in that business, but they hide it pretty well. Buchanan has all the sporting places sewed up."

"My name is Kelly and I'm also married, so I'm not looking for sport. I do want to engage you though. I will give you fifty cents a day for information I may want."

"My, you must be rich. What kind of information?"

"The kind you gave me about Buchanan. Don't ask people about Clark Smith, or it could be detrimental to your health. I wouldn't want that on my conscience."

"I may not look it, but I'm smart. I know how to get information without causing suspicion. I like you, and I like the job you've given me. We seem to fit together, kind of like the Pinkerton agency."

Kelly smiled and said, "Does Buchanan play poker?"

"Yes, but generally with the same players. They're all business men. None of his employees play in that game."

"Where is that game?"

"Here on Saturday night. A lot of people watch the game."

"Who is generally the winner?"

"That's hard to say. There is one business man who seems to always fare better than the others. Buchanan wins occasionally, but really not that often. He makes so much money, that this game means very little to him financially."

"When does the game start?"

"About eight o'clock and lasts until twelve."

"Is anyone allowed to watch them?"

"Sure, though not many do. I watch occasionally, if someone I'm having a drink with wants to watch. It's fun to watch."

"I'll be here tomorrow at eight."

"I'll be waiting for you."

As it was Friday, Kelly was there the next night at eight. The game was just about to start. They stood just far away so they could whisper without being heard, but close enough to see the play. None of the players seemed that sharp accept one. They called him Hank. Lola told Kelly his name was Harold Kapps. He was a man in his fifties, but with premature gray hair. Lola said he ran a waterfront saloon called "The Wake."

Hank did not win every time he dealt, but enough so that Kelly could see him dealing from the bottom, and sometimes, second-card dealing. His game was five card stud poker.

The others mainly liked five card draw. The stakes weren't that high. They played table stakes, with a one hundred dollar buy in. You were allowed to put more money into the game, only if you got below twenty-five dollars. You were then only allowed a hundred dollars, and only one time.

Lola said, "The restrictions were put in by Bill Buchanan to keep people from getting hurt badly. I don't think it would hurt Bill if they played for thousands."

After the game Kelly hung around and asked. "What would it take to get me in that game?"

"You couldn't. However, I have heard of another game that is much bigger. Buchanan knows about it, but never plays in it, I'm told."

"Told by whom?" Kelly asked.

"Sometimes I have a conversation with our manager. He likes me. He knew my husband and knows our circumstances. That is the reason I got the job. It was surely not for my outstanding beauty."

"I don't know, Lola. I find you handsome. I would pick you over the other women, as far as beauty is concerned."

"You're not cutting my pay are you, Kelly," she quipped.

"I was't kidding, I think you're good looking."

Lola said, "You've been away from your wife too long, Kelly," then kissed him on the cheek.

Kelly went to the Wake saloon the next afternoon. Hank was standing at the end of the bar. Kelly just sauntered down the bar, as it was less crowded there. Hank was not the most pleasant person to be around. He was arrogant, and looked with disdain upon others.

Kelly ordered a whiskey. Even though he was standing next to Hank, he didn't engage him in conversation. However, the man on the other side of Kelly asked, "Are you new to Chicago?"

"Yes, I am. Do I look like a dude or something?"

The man laughed and said, "If you do, you are among brothers," and they both laughed.

Kelly then said, "I like to play poker, just for entertainment you know." His drink arrived and Kelly said, "Bring my friend another round, and opened his wallet. It was stuffed with hundred dollar bills, which was not lost on Hank's gaze.

The man next to Kelly thanked him, and after the one drink said, "I hate to run, but I have a meeting in five minutes," and left.

Hank then introduced himself to Kelly. He said, "I heard you tell your friend that you liked to play poker for entertainment. A few of my friends and I play on Tuesday evening upstairs where I have a room just for that."

Kelly said, "That sounds interesting. What are the stakes?"

"They are a little high, but you can quit anytime you want. There are no card sharks there. It's table stakes with a three hundred dollar buy-in."

Kelly whistled, "That's a rich game. I'll try it once, but if it's too rich for my blood, please don't be offended if I leave. I'm fairly well to do, but want to stay that way."

Hank laughed and said, "You'll do okay. Even though the stakes are somewhat high, most of the men don't lose or win that much. However, there is much more excitement when the stakes are high, and isn't that's why most of us play?"

"I never thought about it as that, but I think you have a point. You must be smarter than most of us to have thought that out." This made Hank beam.

Tuesday night Kelly was on time, and was led to a room that appeared to have been built for cards. It had a table that had six sides, and was covered with green felt. There were trays for your coins in front of you for your convenience. A place was also provided for a drink. Three beautiful women were there to attend them.

Kelly was introduced to the other four by Hank who said, "Kelly is new in town, and he likes to play poker. I invited him to play with us since Oliver's wife is ill. So take it easy on him boys. We want him to see Chicago as a nice place to reside."

The game started. Kelly was dealt three kings on the very first deal. He bet them conservatively and won the hand. He folded the next three hands, then the deal was passed to him.

Kelly said, "I never deal. The reason is, that I found I am luckier than most folks, so I pass the deal, so you know I'm not cheating."

The others laughed and a man named Tom said, "I think he's just lazy," and they all laughed. The next time that Hank dealt, he broke out a new deck. The cards were shuffled and cut, but Kelly saw an old trick used. When the dealer asks for a cut, it looks like a cut, but the dealer actually puts the cards back just like they were originally.

The game, which Harold liked particularly, was five card stud. Kelly noticed a bottom deal on the first card Hank dealt to himself. Kelly was given the jack of spades and another jack for his up card. The man to his right had an ace showing and he bet ten dollars. Kelly folded. He could detect a slight surprise on Harold's face. This threw the cards off from what Hank just knew would play out like he wanted. The man to his right ended up winning two hundred dollars from Hank, who ended up with two queens, but the man to Kelly's right had two aces.

It was the biggest hand of the evening. Kelly won his share, and left with an extra hundred dollars. As he was cashing in his coins for folding money, he said, "Just like I told you, I'm just lucky."

Hank still thought Kelly was a mark. Maybe he didn't have the jack he thought was in the hole. He patted Kelly on the back and said, "Can we count on you for next Tuesday?"

Kelly said, "I hope so, but one never knows."

The next night Lola said, "I told one of the girls that a man, who was in here last night, asked if I had heard of a Clark Smith." As Kelly was not there that night, he was safe. The girl she told it to was a close friend of the manager, and asked him when Lola was with them.

The manager got a surprised look on his face and said, "Who was the man, Lola?"

"Just some stranger I had never seen before. He drank one drink, and was gone. If he ever comes back, I'll point him out."

"What's the big fuss, Sam?"

"He was one of Buchanan's men. I got it that he was too familiar with Buchanan's business. He suddenly disappeared, like we all may do, if this gets back to Buchanan." Both girls were startled, and said they would never mention the name again.

Saturday night came. Kelly was already at a place to watch the game when Buchanan and Hank came in. Hank stopped in front of Kelly and said, "You're a friend of the game aren't you Kelly?"

He then turned and introduced Buchanan to Kelly. He said, "Kelly, here, is a fan of the game."

Kelly said, "I'm happy to meet you Mr. Buchanan. I find watching poker as interesting as playing, as you can see all the strategies in motion."

Buchanan said, "I see your point. I never thought about it from a spectator's point of view, but I think you're right. After awhile you would have favorite players such as other sports."

He then turned to Hank and said, "Maybe we should build a small grandstand around the table, so others could see what Mr. Andrews has seen. That's a very interesting perspective, I like it, but not so much that I would drop out from playing," and everyone laughed.

One of the players didn't show up. Buchanan turned and said, "Would you like to join us Mr. Andrew?"

Kelly said, "Thank you Mr. Buchanan," and joined the table.

When it came Kelly's deal he said what he always said, "I'll pass the deal. I'm so lucky at cards that I never deal. That keeps people from thinking I'm cheating."

Buchanan laughed and said, "That is an interesting concept. You are an interesting person, Mr. Andrews. What do you do for a living?"

"Nothing at present. I would say I play poker for a living, but after you see me play, you would know that couldn't be true," and everyone laughed.

"But you must have some income, tell us about yourself."

"Yes, I served in the war for four years. Although in many battles, I came out without a scratch. But, like most of the soldiers, I just wanted to get away from people, so I took a job as a cowboy on a ranch near Springfield, Missouri. I was in the cavalry, so it worked out. I finally was able to diminish the thoughts of the killing I witnessed, so they weren't so vivid. After three years, the owner sold the ranch, and I was out of a job. About that time, I received a small legacy. I decided to just drift and ended up in Chicago playing poker with Hank, here, and you, Mr. Buchanan."

"Well, after knowing your life history, I think we should be on a first name bases. Call me Bill. I want to thank you for your service, as every man in this room should do. I don't know where we would be without men like you. Have a seat, I want to reward you by taking some of your money," and everyone laughed.

Kelly did just like he said, he passed the deal each time. He was unusually lucky and each time said, "I'm just lucky. Sometimes to the point of embarrassment, like tonight." He had only won a hundred dollars as the betting was slight."

Buchanan said, "I would like to know you better, Kelly. Why don't you have dinner with me tomorrow night? Maybe we can talk a little business. You need something to do besides playing poker. I think I can use the excellent mind you possess. You see things others don't seem to perceive."

"I would like that, Bill, when and where."

Bill said, "Where are you staying, Kelly? I'll have my driver pick you up at seven tomorrow night."

Kelly didn't leave with the others. He stayed to talk to Lola. She said, "My, have you worked your way up in the world. I would have bet my grandmother's necklace that you would never get in that game, much less have dinner with Buchanan and call him by his first name."

Sam was standing near to them and said, "I think we ought to run you for president the next time around, Kelly."

Kelly said, "That job is too dangerous for me," and they all laughed.

After Kelly left Sam said, "I can see why you hang around Kelly. He seems to draw people to him. I like him and only know a little about him. Try to find out all you can about him, Lola. He's one we should keep around."

Lola laughed to herself and thought, *"Should I ask Sam for an extra fifty cents a night. I'm turning into a detective."*

The next night Kelly was taken to a place abutting Lake Michigan that protruded out over the water. It was a nice evening. When he arrived Bill said, "I hope you don't mind, but I brought a few girls along to brighten up the place. After I told them about you, all four of them wanted to come meet you. I'm not married, as I'm sure you aren't, so there's no harm done."

As the meal progressed Bill said, "Kelly, I run a large business. I like to think I help the community with the services I provide them. We have very little crime and everyone seems to prosper."

"What exactly do you provide the community, Bill?"

"I insure each business from fire, robbery or any other thing that might beset them."

"So you are the police and fire department. That must save the citizens a lot of money if they don't have to pay for these agencies."

"Not exactly, Kelly. We have a police department and fire department. My service is to see that no one takes advantage of them for just a small fee."

"Why can't the police and fire department do that. Isn't that their job?"

"You are perceptive, Kelly. I provide the citizens insurance, so nothing will happen to them. It gives them piece of mind."

"So, if a store is robbed or a place accidentally burns, you reimburse them?"

"No, but I do help."

"Please don't think I am impertinent, but it seems you are levying a tax on them."

"Yes, I guess I am....for my service."

"What if someone doesn't want your service?"

"All of them do. They see the wisdom of it, and so far, I have had just a little trouble here and there."

"What happens if someone refuses to pay your tax?"

"The police call on them and then they pay."

"I think I get the overall concept, Bill"

"Good, I think you could help me a great deal, Kelly. You see things no one else seems to think of. I would like to engage you as a trouble shooter. I'll point out problems I'm having, and you can provide the solutions. I will pay you twenty-five dollars a week. That should keep you in good cigars for awhile."

"I'll take the position, but unless I really get into it, I can't promise you I will stay. I've found I'm a nomad, and can't stay anywhere too long."

"I think Chicago and the job will grow on you. You will have an office over the Chicago Bank, next to mine. I want to use you as a sounding board on anything we do. You seem to ask the right questions, that gets to the crux of the problem."

After settling into his office, Kelly began learning Buchanan's business. The city was broken into four districts with one of

Buchanan's men in charge of each district. The four lieutenants were men with little to no conscious. Each was used in various vices such as prostitution, a numbers game and picking up the "taxes" Bill levied on merchants. The police chief came in regularly, and always left with a white envelope. The complete city appeared to be under Buchanan's thumb.

There was a book keeping department. Kelly knew that the center of any organization was the finances. The bookkeeping department was run by two brothers, Alvin and Amos Dark. They were men in their early fifties. Kelly decided if he were able to bring Buchanan down, he would have to become close friends with the Dark brothers.

He learned everything he could about them without causing suspicion. He knew they were both married, and their children were grown and on their own. None of the children were connected with Buchanan. They had just one drink at a saloon close to the bank, then went home. Kelly even found out the brand of whiskey they liked.

Kelly mailed a letter every week to Colonel Alfred telling him everything that was going on. The Colonel relayed this information to the attorney general, who then passed it on to the newly elected President Grant. He was told that the information was top secret, as one man had already lost his life, Another could die, if any information were leaked back to Chicago.

Kelly was given a list of merchants who protested the tax that Buchanan levied. He began calling on these merchants. He outlined the services that Buchanan provided. He introduced himself as Buchanan's agent, to the first man he contacted.

He said, "I understand you are opposed to the five per cent tax that Buchanan takes from you. I want to assure you that the money is well spent, and is to your benefit. If you will hear me out, I will outline these services, then you decide if it's of benefit to you.

"Before Buchanan came to Chicago, policemen shook you down for a lot more than Buchanan charges. He stopped the robberies that have occurred, and the gangs that caused all kinds of trouble. The politicians use to raise your property taxes regularly, and you couldn't do anything about it. Since Buchanan came, the police are now doing their job, and your property taxes are stable. Buchanan keeps all of these people in line for your benefit. He can't do this for free. Five per cent is a small part of your gross income, so you are better off money wise. You sleep a lot better now, knowing someone is looking after your interest. I think you owe Mr. Buchanan an apology, and should do so by writing a letter to him. If you want, I will help you do this."

The merchant he talked to thought Kelly had revealed a revelation to him. He had changed his mine and asked Kelly to help him write the letter to Buchanan. It mentioned the services that Buchanan provided and thanked him.

Most of the disturbed merchants saw the wisdom of what Kelly told them, and fell into line. Kelly had business cards printed with his title being, *Agent for Better Government*. He put the address of his office and told the merchants he was available to them, anytime.

One of the people who objected to Buchanan's tax was a restaurant owner. He wouldn't buy anything that Kelly told him. The next week a man from the public health department closed his restaurant. He came hat in hand to Kelly's office the next day. Kelly saw that he was able to reopen the following day.

The letters came into Buchanan's office everyday. Buchanan came to Kelly and said, "I can't believe how good you are. My lieutenants have no enforcing to do, and everything seems to be running much smoother. I'm doubling your salary, and if it continues like this, I may double it again. You're worth more to me than any of my employees. One thing, please don't tell anyone what I pay you. Petty jalousies you know."

CHAPTER 9

THE DARK BROTHERS

While Kelly was doing his job, he met the Dark brothers. They were located just down the hall from his office. He went to their office, and introduced himself. They both knew that Kelly was held in high regard by Buchanan, because he lauded Kelly constantly.

Kelly invited them to his office after work to have a drink with him. Kelly had purchased a bottle of whiskey that was very expensive. It was Irish whiskey, and the best. He poured each of them a drink then said, "The reason I asked you to have a drink with me is to get better acquainted. Whether you realize it are not, you two are the most important employees in this entire organization."

Both men were shocked, as they looked at themselves as just bookkeepers. Kelly said, "The financial part of any organization is its very soul. I would like to understand this vital part of this business, so that I can do my job better. My job is to inform merchants, who are opposed to Buchanan's taxes, to see the benefit that Buchanan provides them. Most see it immediately. Where in the past, merchants were brought into line by intimidation, I have stopped most of that by simply educating these merchants as to the value they receive from Buchanan."

Alvin said, "My lord man, you must have a silver tongue." and all laughed.

Kelly said, "No, it's simply the truth." Kelly then outlined the services that Buchanan provided. They were now on their third drink, and both men were in an excellent mood. Kelly then said, "I would like to know everything about Buchanan's business, so I can do my job better. Will you help me?"

Both men said, "We will do all we can."

Kelly added, "If you don't mind, I think we should keep this just between us, as Buchanan and others may not see it that way. You know how petty jealousies are," and both nodded.

Kelly spent an hour with the Dark brothers each day. It was done the first thing in the morning. Kelly had noticed most of people who worked in the bank building, including Bill Buchanan, came at nine or after in the morning. The Dark brothers were early risers, and were there before eight each day.

In the following weeks Kelly learned of every operation that Buchanan ran. He made a log of each of them that included the amount of cash Buchanan extracted. He was astounded at the amount.

Kelly had stopped sending details of Buchanan's operation, and now just sent a postcard, saying he was still investigating.

Kelly knew he must find out what happened to Clark Smith. He approached one of the soldiers of a certain section. Kelly had said, "One of the merchants asked me if I knew a Clark Smith. I had never heard of him, but to appease the man, I said I would look into it for him."

The soldier looked both ways and said, "Don't say it came from me, but Smith disappeared after Buchanan checked up on him. I hear he is in Lake Michigan wearing concrete shoes."

Kelly said, "Well, I'll just tell the man that Smith left for a better job."

"Smart," the soldier said.

Kelly was now wooing the four lieutenants who ran the four districts. He did this one at a time. He was well liked by all, as Buchanan always had a good word about him.

One evening after work, Kelly asked the Dark brothers if they had a plan for when Buchanan's scheme blew up. They both had shocked faces. Kelly said, "You think this will last forever?"

Alvin said, "I never thought about it, but now that you mention it, I can see your point."

Kelly said, "It just takes one election where a 'do-gooder' comes into clean up crime and corruption. They would hang this around your necks, as you are well aware of all the corruption that is happening here."

Amos said, "We need to keep two sets of books, Alvin. One of them would show only legitimate things."

Kelly said, "There's nothing Buchanan does that is legitimate. Hard cash and a get-away plan is the only thing that will do you any good."

Alvin said, "He's right, Amos. How will we protect ourselves?" he asked almost rhetorically.

Kelly said, "We three need access to the bank vault. I'm told that Buchanan keeps a large amount of cash in the vault, just in case things go south."

"But, how would we have access to it?" asked Alvin.

Kelly said, "I will talk to Buchanan. I'll suggest that you keep the ledgers in the vault as a clever man could steal them."

"Clever man, why we keep the books in a filing cabinet that anyone can open."

"Yes, that's what I'll tell Buchanan. If he allows you to place the ledgers in the vault, you will have access."

"Yes, but there will be the manager or assistant manager with us at all times, so how could we help ourselves?"

"I'll have to think about that for awhile, but that too is solvable."

"You are a dear friend, Kelly. It was a good day when Alvin and I made your friendship."

"The first thing I want you to do, when you are in the vault, is to find out where the cash is. Not gold or coins, as they would be too heavy and awkward to cover up. You must always carry the ledgers in a clothe bag. When you see where they keep Buchanan's cash, you can tote it out in the cloth bags. There must be something to replace the cash, so that it's not missed. I suggest cutting newspaper the size of the bills and then put a bill on the front and back of a wrapped stack."

"Brilliant, Kelly. No one would ever know until they unwrapped a stack of bills, and that wouldn't happen until Buchanan removes them after his get-away."

"None of us should ever talk about this, but we three. It will be our secret. Time is not on our side. The feds could be working on busting Buchanan at any time. Bill knows that too, and I would bet he already has a get-away plan."

Both Dark brothers nodded. They now spent their evenings cutting up newspapers the size of a bill. They even had their wives cutting them up. They explained they needed the cut up newspapers for their work.

Kelly was still playing poker on Friday and Saturday night. He won steadily, but not so much as to alarm the others. Buchanan was always trying to get him to go with some of his many girlfriends. Although Kelly drank and partied with them at times, he never bedded the girls, and never went with the same girl twice in a week.

Kelly made friends with the assistant manager of the bank, Tom Aster. Tom was about Kelly's age. He was going with the bank manager's daughter, Mary. She was plain, but was fancied up with clothes and cosmetics. Tom was not in love with Mary, he just saw her as a prudent step forward. That is how he became assistant manager.

Tom did like to have a drink now and then. Kelly told the Dark brothers that he was going to befriend Tom Aster, and they should not come to his office after work for awhile. Kelly had a knack for making friends. Tom loved his whiskey, as it was free. His boss didn't pay him that well, and Tom was required to take Mary to dinner at expensive places.

Tom and Kelly became close friends. On the days where Tom was told to lock up, Kelly would go downstairs, and talk to him while the Dark brothers put away there ledgers.

The Dark brothers, as well as Kelly, got a good layout of the vault and where the cash was kept.

Kelly came up with a plan, and laid it out for the Dark brothers. He said, "I want you to tell Tom the next time you are putting up the ledgers, that you need a filing cabinets in the vault, as you have many more sensitive books that need to be under lock and key. Tell Tom that you want to move them down to the vault Say you will need his help, as you don't want anyone else to know your books are kept there. Tell him that Amos has a bad back. I will show up the day of the move and during that time, I will keep Tom busy, while you and Amos remove and replace about fifty stacks of bills. Try to put the bogus bills as far back as possible."

It worked. When they returned upstairs they counted out sixty-thousand dollars. Alvin said, "Where shall we keep such cash?"

Kelly said, "In the vault inside the filing cabinets. Put them in cloth bags."

"Will we have time to recover the bags if something comes down in a hurry."

"Who knows, but I'm sure Buchanan will want you to take the ledgers out of the vault and destroy them. He knows you would be implicated as deeply as he is, so he would trust you with that task."

This worked also. Kelly found other ways to distract Tom, when the Dark brothers were in the vault. They soon had over two hundred thousand dollars in the cabinets.

When Alvin told Kelly the filing cabinets were full, Alvin said, "I'll find another hiding place for our cash. We would have to have another filing cabinet if we continue. Kelly thought of a place. He had rented a barn near his apartment. He kept some horses and a buggy there. He had a place underneath a feeding trough that was perfect. The Dark brothers began carrying stacks of cash to him. Kelly had cloth bags to transport the cash to his hiding place.

Kelly said, "If I give you the word, go get all the cash. Keep a hand truck available, and haul the filing cabinets up to your office. You can then take the cash in your clothe bags and leave. I'll see that the ledgers are destroyed, and you will see that you get on a train for New York." This made both brothers smile.

Kelly was again writing Colonel Alfred with details of Buchanan's activities. The justice department had received many letters from merchants of how private citizens were being taxed. They had no one who could hear them, as the police and government officials were in Buchanan's pocket.

A date was set for the raid, and it was given to Kelly. There would be ten men from the attorney general's office with subpoenas to raid the bank building including the vault. The day before the feds arrived, Buchanan was tipped off. He went to the vault, and had his men retrieved all his money. He left that day before the feds arrived. His four lieutenants went with him. He ordered the Dark brothers to burn the ledgers. They retrieved the ledgers, and with their hand truck moved the filing cabinets upstairs, extracted the cash, and left the ledgers with Kelly. The Dark brothers were gone with their money, that amounted to over two hundred thousand dollars.

Buchanan never looked at his money, as it looked just like what had been placed in the vault. He traveled to New York City where he had friends. It was over two months later, that he discovered that he had been cheated out of half his wealth. However, by that time, he was integrated with some of his friends in other schemes. He surmised that the bank manager had bilked him. However, the bank manager had been arrested along with Tom Aster.

The payoffs to the police and fire chiefs were revealed, but they, and several of their underlings had retired and left Chicago. The mayor and several councilmen had turned in their resignations to the city clerk. The whole government structure had crumbled.

As Kelly knew the date and hour the feds would arrive, he had left the day before, also. He left the ledgers in Buchanan's office. He shook the Dark brothers hands and said, "Go out of the country for a few years. I suggest the Bahamas. They have good parties and the climate is nice. They also have all the amenities for the rich."

They took his advice.

Kelly retrieved the money from under the feed trough and it amounted to nearly three hundred thousand dollars. He took this with him, and went to Washington DC. He was paid his two thousand. He told Colonel Alford that he needed a few months off, but would keep him informed about his whereabouts. He also informed him that Clark Smith was probably killed by Buchanan's men. He then headed for New York City.

No stories appeared in the Chicago Tribune, other than many city officials had resigned. New elections were held, new judges and city officials were appointed. The city seemed to go right on functioning as it had, minus Buchanan's tax and several of his illegal ventures.

CHAPTER 10

LEAVING FOR THE WEST

Posing as a cattle buyer from Kansas City, Kelly deposited a hundred thousand dollars in each of two banks. He kept a little less than ninety thousand, and left for Coffeeville. It took him over a week to get there. He had written Patty that he would be there in just over a week.

La Barr tried to get him to stay with him at his ranch, but Kelly said, "We're off to California. That is where Patty wants to go for awhile."

La Barr said, "I don't know where you get the money to not work, and just gad about the country like the very rich."

"I work for a rich uncle. He pays me well."

Patty was excited about the trip. She would have Kelly alone. They arrived at Kansas City, and while Patty was shopping, Kelly used that time to deposit eighty thousand dollars in the Kansas City bank. He decided to keep several thousand as it was more than enough to gamble with, and pay their expenses. He told the bank manager that he would be calling on him to send him money through other banks. He gave him a code word, so the manager would know it was him who was asking for the transfer of money.

They took a riverboat to the railhead that ran to California. The trip was everything that Patty wanted. They stopped over in Omaha, so the trip would not get tedious. It was like a honeymoon for Patty.

Kelly always had his rifle and handgun with him, as he knew the West could be dangerous.

At a place called Julesburg on the Nebraska and Colorado boarder, a celebration was going on. A cattle drive had ended there, and the towns people decided to celebrate. The cowboys left the day after they delivered the herd. However, negotiations were still going on about the cattle price with several buyers.

There was a gang of outlaws, who called themselves the *Wild Bunch*, who followed the herd knowing there would be a huge amount of money in the bank to payoff the owner of the herd.

Not knowing this, Patty wanted to stay for the celebration, as it looked like fun. Kelly rented them a room at the hotel, and they went to dinner. They had a fine wine of which Patty drank several glasses. When they went back to their room, Patty said, "I'm tired and need to go to bed.

Kelly said, "Do you mind me going downstairs. There may be a poker game I could watch."

Patty was really tired. She smiled and said, "Have a good time."

It was now after nine, and a poker game was going on. It was between cattle buyers, and a couple of merchants. Kelly watched for an hour, and by this time he knew the player's habits pretty well. One of the players was tapped out and left. Kelly took this opportunity to ask if he could join them. He was welcomed.

Two hands went by and Kelly had folded both times. The deal was passed to him and he said, "If you don't mind, I never deal unless made to. I get very lucky sometimes, and I don't want to have that happen while I'm dealing."

This brought a lot of laughter. One of the cattle buyers said, "I don't mind dealing for you, it gives me a better opportunity to cheat these fellers," and everyone laughed.

One of the other players said, "Bart, you couldn't stack a deck if we gave you the deck and twenty minutes in the toilet alone," which brought a lot of laughter. Kelly could tell it was a friendly game.

Kelly folded each hand until the sixth hand. He had been dealt three fours. Instead of taking two cards, he took one. It was the case four. There had been lively betting. Kelly had only called the raises. It then came to the man behind him who had also taken one card. The man bet a hundred dollars, which was the highest bet of the evening. Kelly studied his hand for sometime, then called him, because across the table a man who had started the betting had raised each time.

This time, however, the man across the table paused for sometime then said, "I'll see that hundred and raise you another hundred. There was deathly silence as the next man folded. The man who had raised the hundred said, "I'll raise you another hundred. Everyone at the table thought Kelly would fold, as he had never raised, and everyone counted him for hitting a straight. After a long time, Kelly, said, "I'll call. The man across the table said, "I'll call.

The man to Kelly's right laid down a heart flush with an ace, king high. Kelly just sat there, but the man across the table couldn't wait, he laid down a full house. He was about to rake in the money when Kelly laid down his four-fours. Everyone gasped.

Kelly said, "Just like I told you, 'I sometimes get very lucky.'"

The man across the table then hurriedly picked up all the cards and laid them out in suits counting each card. They were all there. Kelly said, "That was very unfriendly of you, neighbor. Only cheaters think others are cheating."

All eyes were now on the man who had counted the cards. He had hate in his eyes and pushed back from the table. Kelly had anticipated this move and already had his derringer in his hand. As the man reached for his gun, Kelly pointed his derringer at the man and said, "Don't get yourself killed over a card game, neighbor."

The man could see Kelly had him dead to rights, and put his hands back on the table. Kelly then said, "You were dealing, not me."

The man then stood and left. One of the men said, "Good riddance."

This broke up the card game. The man who had the flush said, "You are lucky. Are you a card shark?"

"No, like I say, I'm just lucky, and wait for an opportunity."

"Yes, I saw you fold more times than anyone. Why didn't you raise me after the last raise?"

"Like you said, 'This is a friendly game,' and I don't like to see anyone hurt. I play for the fun of the game. My greatest pleasure is watching the game. Sure, I like to win, but I lose, also. If you didn't lose, it wouldn't be fun. It's the excitement of the game that's fun, whether you are playing for nickels and dimes or dollars. I will say that was the most expensive hand I have ever played."

"Well, everyone is flush after the cattle drive. Tomorrow is the biggest game. That's when we settle with the herd owner, and the bidding begins. That game is for high stakes"

"Yes, I can see this game is penny-ante compared to that one." Kelly then stuck out his hand and said, "Good luck."

Kelly and Patty's train was due to leave at nine in the morning. They had their bags packed, and had eaten a good breakfast. They were just stepping out the door going to the train station, when they heard the yells of men riding their horses in a gallop coming into town. They had their revolvers out, and were shooting up the town. They shot out glass store windows, and everything they thought would scare people. Kelly caught Patty, and was pulling her toward the door when a bullet hit Patty in the head. She never knew what hit her.

Kelly could tell she was dead, and just pulled her into the lobby of the hotel, and laid her on a sofa. He then opened his suitcase, and retrieved his gun and holster. He took their luggage back upstairs. He broke out his rifle from its case, along with a box of cartridges. He went to a window and peered out. The riders were still shooting up the town. The sheriff came out with two deputies, and began shooting at the riders. They hit one of the gang, but then were all shot dead.

Kelly opened his window and screwed the silencer on his rifle. He stood back from the window enough so no one could see him, and shot one of the riders. He then shot another. The riders could hear nothing, but their own pistols. They were now looking everywhere. Kelly shot another, and then the riders got off their horses, and took cover.

Kelly put his rifle back in its case and took it to the hallway. There he saw what he was looking for, an access to the attic. He brought a chair from his room and lifted the access panel and slid the rifle case into the attic. He then climbed down and went to his room and retrieved the suitcase with his money, and carried it to the chair, and put his money in the attic, also. He replaced the panel, and took his chair back to his room. He knew there would be a search, and he didn't want to be there when that happened.

Kelly went to a window at the end of the hall. He could see another building close to the hotel with a narrow space, maybe three or four feet wide, between buildings. He lowered himself out the window, then dropped down. The narrow space led to an alley. He could see the back corral of the livery stable, and made his way there. He had just arrived when he saw two of the riders coming down the alley. Kelly shot them both with his pistol that had its silencer on. He then walked up to them, and shot both in the head. He drug the two men to the narrow space between the buildings, and put them there. He covered them with boards he found in the alley.

Kelly went into the livery stable. He saw a frightened hostler looking out the front of the barn. Kelly said, "Who are those men?"

The hostler said, "My boss said they were the *Wild Bunch*. They have robbed other communities. They take anything they want. They take the young women to the saloon, and make them do terrible things. No one can match them, as there are too many.

"Well, someone must be fighting them, I see several in the street dead and none of them are on the street now."

"That may be true, but I would hate to be that man, when they catch up to him."

Kelly smiled to himself and began looking around. There was a church that sat about a five hundred feet from the bank. Kelly could see that from the bell tower, he would have a full view of the bank's and saloon's front doors. He told the hostler that he was getting out of town.

The hostler said, "I would too, if I had anywhere to go." Before leaving, Kelly went by a saddle that had a canteen on it. It was full. He looked into the saddle bags and they contained a lot of jerky. He put all the jerky he could carry in his pockets, and left.

Kelly went to the backdoor of the hotel. It was locked, so he took his foot and kicked it open. No one was around, as all were at the front of the hotel looking out the windows. He went up the stairs and retrieved his rifle and a box of cartridges. He then went back out the backdoor, and down the alley that led to the church. He was able to get in the backdoor of the church, as it was unlocked. There was a ladder that led up to the belfry. He had to make two trips to get his rifle, a chair and the canteen to the belfry platform. He looked down the street, and it was empty. He sat on the chair, and rested his rifle on the ledge of the belfry.

The street was empty for an hour or two. It was then Kelly had time to reflect on what had happened. He was sorry Patty was dead, but he was not overwhelmed with grief like some men who lost a wife. He then thought of their relationship. Was it only lust that made him love Patty. He knew she loved him more than he loved her, but then in nearly all relationships, they're not even.

He thought, *"Have I killed so many men that I have lost desire for another human?* He then thought of the men he had met in the past four years. None were really close to him. He liked them, but if he never saw them again, it wouldn't really matter. This really alarmed him. Was he like others he knew, who cared for no one other than themselves?

Kelly shook this off, because he did care for other people. That is why he was bent on keeping the people safe in Julesburg. Maybe he was just doing it for revenge for them taking something that belonged to him. He did love Patty. Maybe he wasn't crazy in love with her, like some men he had known. That happened mostly during the war. Men wanted to hang onto something, which intensified their love. He didn't have a love at that time, and he looked back over his past relationships. Other than Patty, those were superficial. He had left them without even thinking of them. He vowed he would never do that again. He wanted to love, and have good friends. He had liked the Dark brothers and even thought of them sometimes. He liked to think of them sunning themselves on the beach with a rum and cola in their hands.

He then thought about Leland La Barr. He knew he had to bring Patty's body back to him. He would be devastated. He needed to stay with him awhile, until he was okay.

After noon, two men came out of the saloon and headed toward the bank. Kelly took careful aim and shot one, then the other.

It was eerie to the rest of the *Wild Bunch,* as they were now down to six. The leader said, "There is someone who can kill, but makes no noise."

One of the others said, "Maybe it's the hand of God taking us down. No rifle can shoot without making a sound. There's something terribly wrong here, and I for one say we call it a day, and ride out of here."

Another said, "That goes for me too. There are other towns. We are down to six that we know of. Bill and Rufus just disappeared."

The leader said, "I hate to leave all that money in the bank, but I agree. There are many other towns."

They left out the backdoor of the saloon, and made their way down the alley where their horses were tied. It was now dusk, and they walked their horses to the end of town. They then rode as fast as they could for about a mile.

Kelly had seen them ride, and was able to get one more shot off. It hit the last rider. The others didn't even hear or see him go down.

Kelly knew he had to take Patty home. He came down from the belfry and walked back to the hotel. People were now coming out onto the street. One man asked him if he knew how the bandits were taken down. Kelly said, "It must have been the hand of God. Those were evil men. However, only five rode out. Their number diminished considerably. Maybe they will think twice before they ride into another town."

The man said, "The hand of God. I believe it. There never was a shot. They just dropped in their tracks. I think I will tell this to the editor of the paper. Kelly collected Patty and carried her to the undertaker.

The undertaker said, "There are several ahead of you." Kelly held out a hundred dollar note and said, "Will this take her to the head of the line?"

The undertaker said, "I see your lady as a priority."

Kelly said, "I want her embalmed, and put in the finest coffin you have."

"You'll have it, Sir. She will be ready tomorrow morning."

Kelly went to the train station and asked when the first eastbound train would be there the next day. It was eight the next morning. He bought his ticket, and said there would be a coffin to come aboard. Kelly got everything ready. He recovered his money, his and Patty's luggage and his firearms. It took him over a week to get back to La Barr's ranch.

Kelly had rented a wagon, and had Patty's coffin on it. He drove up to the front of La Barr's house, and he came out. He saw the coffin and fell to his knees. He didn't cry outwardly, but his whole body shook. Kelly pulled him up and held him. They both kept clinched for a minute or two. Finally La Barr said, "Help me bring Patty into the dining room. We will lay her casket on the dining room table."

After that was done, La Barr opened the casket. The undertaker had done a marvelous job. Patty looked just like she was asleep. He had patched the hole in her head so well, you could hardly tell it was there.

La Barr then asked, "What happened?"

Kelly said, "Come into the living room. Do you have some whiskey?"

La Barr went and retrieved a quart of brandy and two glasses. He poured Kelly's drink, and Kelly related the complete story as best he could. He then said, "I killed eleven of those bastards before they ran out of town. I will stay a week with you, but I won't rest until every jack man of them are below ground."

"I want to go with you Kelly."

"I do better alone, Leland."

"Well, we either go together or separately, because I'm going after them, too. I can't live knowing they're still alive."

"Please don't come with me, Leland. I work much better alone. I'm a government agent, and have been trained to do a job like this. If you come, I will have to look out for you, and that will hinder my hunt."

La Barr thought a minute, then said, "I guess you're right, Son. The anger kept me from thinking straight. Of course you'll work better alone. Will you write me a postcard to let me know how you're doing?"

"I'll do that, Leland."

They had a funeral for Patty, and everyone in Coffeyville came. There was much crying and mourning. Richard Thomas came up to Kelly and said, "I'm so sorry, Kelly. I really am. I loved Patty, but she loved you more. After accepting that, I wanted what was best for Patty. We both grieve for her."

Kelly couldn't answer as tears boiled from his eyes. Richard then put his arm around him and said, "I want to hear what happened. I know you can't do it for awhile, but please tell me sometime." Kelly nodded.

La Barr, like most hardened men from the west, had a frozen face. They laid her by her mother in a cemetery by the church.

CHAPTER 11

THE TRAIL OF THE OUTLAWS

Kelly left the next day. It was raining, but he left anyway. He hadn't even thought how he would track these men. All he knew was, they were called the *Wild Bunch* and had robbed towns, trains and stagecoaches.

As he rode he thought, *"There has to be a pattern. If I get a map of the West, I can then put down every place they've robbed the last few years, and try to see a pattern to it. I think Marshal Dobbs can help me. He lives in Topeka. I'll start there."*

It took him a few days to get to Topeka. He went to a hotel first, and had a hot bath, and a change of clothes. He then found Marshal Dobb's office.

Marshal Dobbs was in his office, and put on a smile when he saw Kelly. He stood and stretched out his hand and asked, "Did you bring down Farewell?"

"He's not who you think he is, Marshal Dobbs. I'm not at liberty to tell you what function he does for the government, but just know that he's with them. I hope you will never disclose that to anyone."

"Of course I won't. Why are you calling on me?"

"I know you've heard of the *Wild Bunch*. My wife and I were in Julesburg when they came there. A stray bullet from their guns killed my wife. I want to find them. I want a map of the West, so I can plot their every crime with a date, and what they robbed. There must be a pattern, and if I can decipher that, then I may be able to plot their next move."

"Wow, you are a good detective. I'll get you the map, and the data you want. Where are you staying?"

"At the hotel near the train station, room 205. I'll be waiting for your message. By the way, do you know a good place to eat?"

Dobbs said, "Go to Ma Wilson's boarding house. I think she has the best food in town."

Kelly left, as he had missed a meal as it was. Dobbs was right. Ma Wilson served a family style meal of roast beef and mashed potatoes. The gravy was splendid, and she had hot rolls and three different vegetables."

Kelly stuffed himself. A nicely dressed man next to him asked him where he was from.

Kelly replied, "Coffeeville." Then asked, "Do you know if there is a good poker game somewhere?"

The man said, "I have heard there is one at Marcum's Saloon. However, I have never been there, as I am a pastor."

"Thanks, Reverend," and Kelly took his leave. He found Marcum's easy enough and entered. Near the back he could see a poker game going on. He ordered a whiskey, and went near the game, which was adjacent to the bar. He sat on a bar stool that was high enough so he could see the game quite well.

There were six in the game. It seemed to be an average staked game. The highest bet he saw was for two dollars. They had just started the game. He observed it for over an hour. No one at the table appeared to be a card shark.

A saloon girl had eyed him, and came over and stood by him. He turned and smiled, but didn't address her.

She said, "Are you new in town?"

Kelly nodded, then said, "Is this the best poker game in town?"

She said, "I don't know, but I'll try to find out."

Kelly said, "Would you like a drink?"

She nodded, and the bartender had heard Kelly. He came down and poured her a drink. Kelly paid and she said, "How about sitting at a table?" Kelly had lost interest in the game, as it wasn't very interesting. He nodded, and she led them to a table that was by itself.

After they were seated she said, "My name is Nora Jones," and looked at Kelly with large brown eyes. Her face was made up with rouge and lipstick. She had put some light blue color about her eyes.

Kelly said, "My name is Kelly Andrews. Tell me about yourself."

She smiled and said, "I grew up in Kansas City. When I was eighteen I was swept off my feet by a cowboy. He talked me into going with him. I hated Kansas City, and the man who was living with mother. So, I went with him. He told me he was about to come into a large amount of money. His brother had joined an outfit called the *Wild Bunch*. His brother told him he could make a lot of money if he joined them. He took me here and left me in a hotel with an unpaid bill. I had no way to make a living, so I asked for a job here. That was over a year ago.

About a month ago I read where there had been an attempted robbery by the *Wild Bunch* at a place called Julesburg. He and his brother's names were among those killed. I don't think I loved him that much, because I felt no sorrow.

"It's not so bad here. I enjoy entertaining men. I guess I was born for this kind of life, unless someone like you asks me to go with him. I will demand some upfront money this time, so I don't get stranded."

"Well, Nora, I'm on job to track down men like the *Wild Bunch*. Would you have any idea where they may be headed?"

She thought a minute and said, "He mentioned following the cattle drives. I don't know why and how that could make him any money."

Kelly then got up, smiled at her and left. As he walked to his hotel, he thought, *"How do women get in that fix. It must be a terrible life to have to sleep with anyone off the street."*

The next morning he was in Dobbs' office at eight o'clock. Dobbs had a map for him. He had plotted all the known robberies with their dates on them. Kelly thanked the marshal, and went back to his room. He studied the map all morning. He did find a pattern of sorts. From this he saw that the *Wild Bunch* were headed westward. He found that they picked on towns that weren't too large, as to have a lot of peace officers. The last place they had robbed was at Abilene, Kansas. The railroad now came there, so the cattle drives went there.

Kelly took the train to Abilene. That night he studied his map. When he arrived at Abilene he interviewed a dozen people, who had witnessed the *Wild Bunch,* and what they did. He found there number had grown to ten. They had robbed the bank, and killed two men. One was the banker's son, who braced them during the hold up. He had killed one of them, but lost his life shortly after.

Kelly asked the sheriff of Abilene if he had any notion of where the *Wild Bunch* might be going. The sheriff stroked his chin a couple of times and said, "I think they'll go west. Most outlaws give Texas a wide berth. Those Texans seem to be quite hostile to thieves, and will lose their lives holding them off. The outlaws know this, and ride shy of Texas."

"That's interesting. If more people did that, there would be much less robberies."

"I think you're right. However, people get so used to the easy life, they don't want to risk themselves. So, they just do whatever the bandits ask them to do. I think the *Wild Bunch* will follow a cattle drive. They know that at the end, there will be a lot of money in the bank. Not knowing where the cattle are heading for, they just follow them. I have thought carefully about this, and think that's what they'll do. The cattle drive ended here, and a day later we were hit. I lost a deputy, and the bank lost a man."

Kelly thought about this. He knew a lot of drives would now end at Dodge City, Kansas, because the railroad had just been completed to there. He decided that Dodge would be his next stop.

He arrived at Dodge City three days later. He had thought of nothing but what he would do when he arrived. He rented a room at the Dodge House. He signed the register as Andrew Kelly. The next day, he began scouting the town to see the best place he could be to have an excellent view of the bank.

He found the tallest building in Dodge City. It was a three storied office building with a steep roof. It also had a view of the bank. It had an attic that had three dormers that protruded outward for looks. Kelly went to the owner of the building, who had an office on the first floor. His secretary was in an outer office. Kelly asked to speak to the manager, and was shown into an elaborate office.

Kelly stuck out his hand and said, "I'm Andrew Kelly. I noticed that you have an attic. I have some sensitive material that I would like to store in one of the gables that overlooks the street."

"What does your material contain, Mr. Kelly?"

"They are paper files that I want to make sure no one has easy access to."

"That is an unusual request. There's nothing stored in the attic, except some furniture. I can let you have a space in one of the gables for ten dollars a month. Would that do you?"

"The price is okay, but I would like to see the space."

The owner walked up the steps with Kelly. It had a lock on the door, and the manager used his key to open it. It was somewhat dusty, but the light from the dormers gave them sufficient light to walk to one of them. The windows were five feet high and provided much light. Kelly opened the windows, as there were two windows, actually, that opened like French doors.

Kelly then said, "Would you care if I had the attic cleaned at my expense. It's dusty, and I may have to work here at times."

"By all means, please be my guest. It will be good to air out this place, and have it cleaned. If you need any assistance, please, just let me know."

"There is one other thing. I would like just you and I to have a key. Is there anyone else who has a key?"

"Yes, I have a janitor who has one. I will collect it from him, and give it to you. That way we both win, for I won't have to have a key made for you."

Kelly said, "Could you have your janitor and a helper clean the attic?"

"Yes. He will probably charge you a dollar, though."

Kelly pulled out his wallet and handed the owner eleven dollars. He then said, I will be here tomorrow evening. Will that give your man enough time?"

"Yes, of course. He has two half-grown sons who will help him."

Kelly returned the next evening an hour before dusk. The attic was spotless. He had brought a suitcase and his rifle that was in a case, and that also was contained in a large cloth bag. He was given a key, and made his way to the attic. He was pleased as the attic was clean. He used part of the furniture that was stored. He dragged over a bookcase that was about four feet high. He then carried a straight chair over, so he could sit on it, and lay his rifle over the empty bookcase to steady it if he needed to shoot. The windows were wide enough so he could sit on a soft chair and eye the street while putting his feet on a foot stool. There was a small table he could set beside the soft chair, so he could place a drink or a book on it. He didn't think the *Wild Bunch* would come at night, so he was never there after dark.

He inquired around and found that cattle buyers were arriving from back East. Most of them liked to play poker, so he watched the game at night. The stakes of the game were much higher. The local players dropped out, and became spectators.

As they played Kelly asked, "When do you expect the herd to arrive?"

One of the buyers said, "One of the drovers rode in today, and said they would be here tomorrow. Then the real game begins among us," and they all laughed.

The next day Kelly had brought several sandwiches and a canteen of water. He figured it would be afternoon before the cattle arrived, and he was right. However, he was in his chair eyeing the street after he had his breakfast. The sheriff knew there was danger with that much money in the bank. He had hired extra deputies, and the railroad had furnished some of their detectives to safeguard the money when it arrived in town. The sheriff had put men in strategic locations. Some of them were on buildings.

Men began drifting into town. Kelly thought that these men were probably part of the *Wild Bunch*. They didn't go to the saloon. They just milled around looking at different buildings. Kelly had a good view of the tops of buildings. He thought maybe the *Wild Bunch* was scouting the buildings, and were sent to take out the sheriff's men on building, before they tried to rob the bank. Kelly had the windows wide open, and could see a man going up a building. The man called to the guard and said, "The sheriff sent me to give you a hand."

The guard said, "Find you a place. He then turned back to look down the street. The man pulled a knife, and was within three feet of the guard when Kelly pulled the trigger. The man fell to the ground. The guard turned around as he heard the man fall with his knife in his hand. He realized how close he had come from losing his life. He looked around wondering how the man died.

Kelly killed four other men who had come up the buildings to kill the guards. All men on the buildings were still in place. About an hour later, a group of men came galloping into town shooting their guns at anyone who was on the streets. The five men on the building along with Kelly began the slaughter. Just a few were now alive, and they made it to cover.

He heard the sheriff call out to them. "You can come out with your hands up, or we'll just starve you out. I have twenty men who can out wait you. Either come out now, or we'll just wait and kill you when you have to come out. If you wait, we'll kill you whether you surrender or not.

A few minutes later, three men came out. Each had a woman with a gun to their heads. The leader said, "If you fire on us, we'll kill your women."

Kelly took careful aim, and the leader dropped. Seconds later, another dropped, then the third. No one had heard a thing. Two other men came out with their hands up. Both fell like the others with their chests red with blood. The sheriff's men were in awe.

One of the sheriffs men said, "Just like in Julesburg, the hand of God has struck them down." There were nineteen of the *Wild Bunch* who rode into Dodge City. None were now alive.

Kelly began putting the furniture back and closed the windows. He went by the owner's office. He had just come out from under his desk. Kelly handed him the key and said, "This town is too dangerous to be in, I'm moving on. Just keep the money, I just want out of here."

The owner said, "I don't blame you. I thought I was a goner when I heard all that gunfire."

Kelly left the next day. He bought a paper and the headlines were, "THE HAND OF GOD STRIKES DOWN THE WILD BUNCH."

He then returned to Topeka and called on Marshal Dobbs. When he entered his office, Marshal Dobbs picked up a newspaper that had the headlines in bold type. He said, "When I read this, it struck me who the hand of God was. I don't know how you did it, and don't want to know. I just know that somehow you made this happen."

Expressionless, Kelly said, "I don't know what you're talking about, Sheriff."

The sheriff handed the paper to Kelly. He whistled when he read the headlines. My gosh, it must have taken thirty or forty men to do that. It says here that the last two men gave up, but they were struck down without a sound. How could that be?"

The marshal then thought, *"He really doesn't know."* So, he answered, "Well, maybe you didn't have anything to do with this. Don't matter. Your job is over.

"Where are you headed?"

"Back to Coffeyville, I guess. I have no place else to go."

CHAPTER 12

A SURPRISE ROMANCE

Kelly reached the La Barr ranch, and Leland was glad to see him. The first thing he said was, "I see that the sheriff in Dodge City killed all of the *Wild Bunch*. I was glad to see Patty avenged. She meant so much to me."

"Yeah, she talked about you so much that I gathered she thought a lot about you, also. She loved your humor and told several stories over and over. We both like to hear them even though we both had heard them several times. So you see, we brought you along with us everywhere we went. I'm glad your wife and Patty are lying next to one another. I bet they had a great relationship."

"Yes, but Patty was only ten when God called mama home. If I hadn't had Patty, I think I would have shot myself. She was a good one wasn't she?"

Kelly didn't say anything for awhile and then said, "You know the best time I ever had with Patty?"

Leland looked up and said, "Tell me about it."

"It was the afternoon and night we were tied up together. They tied us so our lips touched each others. Every time we talked, it was like kissing her. I bet she kissed me a hundred times that night. I have thought about that night every night of my life since."

"Well, when you two talked about Harold at the church that day, I never will have a laugh that good again. I still wake up at night laughing. I could just picture you two tied up naked and how it affected you. That Patty could take anything that was terrible, and turn it into something you loved. I wouldn't trade that time in the church for fifty more years of life. I caught on nearly immediately. You two couldn't have made it more funny if you had a week to work on it. I can see why that night was your most pleasant. My, how I miss her.

"I get so lonely at times that I go into town a couple of times a week. They have three new girls at the saloon. I like one of them a lot, as she spends time with me. She acts like she likes me a lot, but then again that's her job."

Kelly said, "Why don't I hook up the buckboard, and go to town. I'd like to have a look at those new girls. I would bet they're as ugly as a mud pie fence," and they both laughed.

As they drove into town, Leland told how he was in the saloon the first night. He said, "The night you and Patty left, I drove into town because I was so lonely. One of the girls, named Linda, hit it off with me that first night. I hate to admit it, but I have gone into town twice a week just to see her. She has a marvelous sense of humor."

They drove in, and were at the bar looking over the new girls. Kelly shook his head and said, "You've been out at that ranch too long, Leland."

Leland had just taken a drink, and sprayed it all over the bar as he laughed. He then said, "I thought I had a sense of humor, but you have one too."

Just then one of the girls came over and said, "Hi, La Barr, is this your brother?"

Leland turned to Kelly and said, "She will have all my money before we leave the bar. She already knows my soft parts."

"Yeah, that's the problem with you. Your soft parts stay that way. I bet your brother here doesn't have that problem."

"Probably not, Linda, but then he's my son-in-law."

Linda said, "Oh, I heard about your wife. I'm awfully sorry."

"Thanks, Linda. I can see why Leland likes you so much, you have a tender heart."

She put her arm around Leland and said, "Leland. So that's your name." She turned to Kelly and said, "He told us his name was La Barr. I figured that was to hold us off from him. However, I aim to make him my boyfriend. I need to put a little life into him, and make him a few years younger."

"I think you are well on your way doing that. Leland has been a widower for over ten years, and should be having a little female company now and then."

While she had his arm around Leland, she turned and looked at him very sincerely and said, "Would you marry me, Leland."

"See, Leland said, "I left most of my money at home, so she wouldn't get it all."

Kelly said, "Of course he'll marry you, Linda. Do you like ranch life?"

"I could learn to love it, I can cook, mend and clean a house, but those aren't my best talents."

Laughing Leland said, "I'm engaged, Kelly, and didn't have a thing to say about it."

Linda then looked at Leland and said, "I was serious. I would marry you tomorrow, Leland."

"Wouldn't you miss the life of having a party every night?"

"We would have a party every night, Leland, I guarantee you that."

"Why don't you take her on a trial bases, Leland. She could come to work for you keeping the house, then see how it goes."

Leland said, "Is everybody serious about this?"

Both Kelly and Linda said, "Yes," at the same time."

Linda said, "You wait here, I'm going to pack my suitcase and tell Sam I had a better offer."

She left and Leland turned to Kelly and said, "What have you gotten me into, Kelly?"

"A great life, I hope. You just hired yourself a housekeeper, and it may work into more."

"Well, I'm lonely most of the time. Even if it doesn't work out, what have I lost?"

"Exactly. She might not be the prettiest thing in town, but she makes up for it with her personality."

"See here, Kelly, you're talking about my fiancé," and they both laughed.

Linda returned, and they put her suitcase on the buckboard, and they were off. When they arrived, Leland showed her the house and her room. It had been a spare room for many years.

Linda said, "You mean I have to sleep alone?"

"Let's play this easy, Linda. If it looks like this works out, maybe we'll get hitched. However, a young girl like you may get tired of me pretty quick."

"I don't think so, but I guess you're right." She then added, "Well, at least until your son-in-law is gone," and they all laughed.

Kelly left the next day and said, "I have to get back to Washington DC. I received a postcard asking me to return. If something serious comes along, just write me at this address and he handed Leland the postcard.

Linda took it and said, "My, you are a big shot."

Kelly decided to take a different way this time. He wanted to go through Joplin and see how Betty Kelly was. He thought of her some.

He decided to ride up to St. Louis, after he spent a day or so in Joplin. He arrived, and went to a barbershop to have a bath and clean up. He went to a clothier first and bought some new clothes, new boots and a new felt hat. He then bathed, had a shave and a haircut. By this time, it was time for supper. He went to a new restaurant called Le

Restaurant. It was run by a French woman named Marie Follet. The meal was the best he had ever eaten, so he asked one of the waitresses who the cook was. He was ushered to the kitchen and said, "Madam Follet, after eating your fine cuisine, I would be remiss if I didn't complement you."

The woman smiled and said in a heavy French accent, "Merci, Monsieur. I am glad you enjoyed my cuisine."

Kelly then went to the saloon and stood at the end of the bar. He could see Betty telling one of her girls about something. He just stood there at the end of the bar that gave him a view of the front door. He was looking at his brandy thinking of the time he spent with Betty when she sidled up to him, and put her arm around him.

She said, "I thought you had left your woman in the port of Joplin, Sailor."

"I could never forget you after the first night we were together."

She said, "Let's go up to my room and you can tell me what happened to you the past two years."

"Has it been that long? Well, I have lived a lifetime during that time. I was married to a wonderful girl, however, she was killed a few months ago in Julesburg by the *Wild Bunch*. She is now buried next to her mother and the *Wild Bunch* are no more."

"Yes, I read about that. They said that all of them died. They said it must have been the hand of God."

"Yes, I suppose it was, or either someone helped God some."

"Are you still in mourning?"

"I loved her, but I was never head over heels like some people get. I will miss her because she was such a fine person, and loved me dearly. As I recall, I think I loved her mostly because she was so in love with me."

Betty said, "That's you alright. You seem to always do the right thing. If I ever married you, I would make you swear on the Bible that you were madly in love with me. However, I think our relationship is just friendship with a lot of lust thrown in."

They talked some more then Kelly said, "I have to turn in, I had a long day today."

Betty didn't ask him to stay as, she knew it was too early, after what had happened to his wife.

Kelly thought as he left, *"Talking to Betty was nice, she is so level headed. I surely like her."*

The next day before he left. He came by and told Betty he was due to check in with his boss, then left.

CHAPTER 13

HOUSTON

Kelly was headed for St. Louis. He had decided to catch a riverboat down the Mississippi River. He always enjoyed the trip, as it was smooth and the food was excellent. He watched more poker than he played. He noticed several card sharks who were really good. There were three of them, and they seemed to take turns being the big winner. Kelly surmised they were partners.

As he traveled, he had time to think. He asked himself, *"Where am I going? What will I do? I'm not overly lonesome, but I seem to have no purpose since Patty is gone. When she was alive, I enjoyed pleasing her. She was an excellent companion. I need someone, but whom? Surely not any of the saloon girls I met."*

He then thought of Leland and Linda. *"They were an odd couple, but each wanted someone, and they happened to meet. Was that how it happens, by accident? Where would I go to meet someone I want to travel through life with?"* The thought was perplexing. He thought that if he could stay someplace for awhile he might be able to meet someone.

He had received a postcard from Colonel Alfred that said he wasn't needed at the time, so he decided to go to Texas. He had never been there, but had heard a lot about it. When he reached New Orleans, he caught a ship to Houston. He had read where the Indians of Texas were mostly confined in North Texas.

When he reached Houston, he stayed in the best hotel they had. He decided to talk to the manager of the hotel about the society there.

The manager's name was Winston Wallace. He was a well dressed man in his early fifties. He asked Kelly, "How may I help you, Mr. Andrews?"

"I'm not sure, Mr. Wallace. I'm new in town. I would like to see Houston, as it may be where I want to live."

"What do you do, Mr. Andrews?"

"Actually nothing. I was left a legacy, and seem to be just ambling through life since my wife died a few months ago. I decided I needed to settle down someplace. I had never been to Texas, so I came here to see how I like it. I have no family, as I lost all of them to the war. It's ironic that I came through all that fighting with men dying all around me, and then find out my mother, father and two sisters were killed during a cannon barrage.

"I left the cavalry after the war and came west where I caught on as a cowboy near Springfield, Missouri. It was exactly what I wanted. Mostly alone, and with simple tasks. The work was hard, but that suited me fine. I wanted nothing to think about, but what was in front of me. I slept better, knowing the killing and slaughter were behind me.

"However, after three years, the owner sold the ranch, and the new owner had his own crew. I had lived a life of solitude enough, and was now ready to start a new life.

"I went west again and miraculously met my wife during a bank robbery. It was so traumatic, that we had a common bond. We became enamored and married. I worked with the government for awhile, but grew tired of that.

"My wife was killed by a stray bullet when neither of us thought we were in any danger. I took her back to her father, who owns a ranch. He was as heart broken as me. I didn't want to stay around where everything reminded me of her, so I came to Texas.

"I'm sorry I laid all that on you, I don't know what came over me."

"Don't be sorry. It was fascinating to hear your story. My wife and I live just a few blocks from here. She is nearly an invalid now, with her joint pains. I would like very much if you would have dinner with us tonight. She sees very few people, now that she is house bound. I think it would do her a lot of good to have dinner with a handsome young man.

"We have a French cook that I pay twice the going rate just to keep her. Other than my devotion to Sara, eating excellent cuisine is my greatest pleasure. I think I know you better than any of my friends that I have known for years. You have bared your soul to me, and I feel you are already a dear friend."

"Thank you Mr. Wallace, I will enjoy having dinner with you and your wife."

"Good, it's settled. Please come by my office a little after five, and we can walk to my house. That's all the exercise I get, so I enjoy the walk."

As they walked to Winston's house, he told how he met his wife and about their two children, who both lived in Austin and worked for the state.

They arrived, and Winston introduced his wife and the cook, Marie. Kelly could tell that Winston and Sara loved Marie because she ate with them. Winston told how he had met Kelly just that day, and they seemed to hit it off. He explained that Kelly was looking for a place to settle down. He further said, he wanted to introduce Kelly to Houston's society.

Sara said, "You came at an excellent time, Mr. Andrews. We received an invitation to a debutant ball in the mail today. As Winston rarely attends these, because I can't attend, you can get him out and about. It will be good for him. I will probably enjoy hearing about the ball more than attending it."

Kelly stayed just a half hour after dinner. He told Marie she was an artist, much like any of the masters.

Marie said, "I hope to see you quite often, Mr. Andrews. You have turned my head," and they all laughed.

The ball was much bigger than Kelly had thought. There were hundreds of people there, all dressed elegantly. Winston introduced him to many people, but then was engaged by three men. Kelly wander away to a bar that was serving drinks.

He turned his back to the bar, and was watching as a handsome man, about his age, was addressing a small group. Standing beside him was a gorgeous woman with a bored look on her face. As his eyes gazed at her, she looked up and they made eye contact. She stared at him as he stared at her. She never dropped her eyes. After just a few seconds Kelly felt self-conscious, and looked back at Winston. He was still engaged with the three men. He then looked back. The woman was still looking at him. He thought, *"Maybe she knows me. She couldn't be that fascinated with the likes of me."*

Just then, she walked directly toward him. She just pushed people aside as her husband never missed a beat, and hardly noticed that she was leaving. This made Kelly very uncomfortable, as she walked toward him. She never looked away.

***

Cali Clayton was born in Boston to an investment broker. Her mother and father had little to do with their children, Cooper and Cali. Their father was gone most of the time on business, and their mother was rapt in society. They had a nanny, but the nannies left, and new ones would come. From a very early age, Cooper and Cali bonded, as they could see all they really had was one another.

Cooper had black eyes that were unusually bright. That was his most outstanding quality. He loved to play games. When he was young he liked to play marbles, and was quite good at it. His prize possession was his taw, an agate. It was a little larger than most marbles, and he could shoot it with his thumb straight and hard.

When they were in their teens, Cooper told Cali that he had hidden his agate, and if she could find it that day, he would buy her a nickel ice cream cone. He said that he had left her a written clue that would help her. It was hidden, and she had to find it.

Cali looked and looked. She looked on every wall and ceiling. She just happened to be in the bathroom doing her business, when she looked above the doorsill inside the bathroom. She could barely make out something. She stood on the commode, and then could see very minutely carved, P. and P. The letters were just above the trim of the door, and to see them clearly, one had to stand on something.

Cali knew at once that this was the clue, even though it was so tiny. She sat on a chair for over an hour, wondering what P. and P. stood for. At last she thought of pots and pans. She raced to the cupboard that housed these, and took everyone of them out, but no agate. She was about to put them back in the cupboard when she took her hand, and wrapped it around the corner of the cupboard, and touched the agate. It was the happiest moment of her life. She put the pots and pans back, and didn't say anything.

Each day they would have a treat at three in the afternoon. Cali was sitting in her usual spot at the kitchen table, and Cooper was to her left. He asked her how the hunt was coming along.

She turned to him and had a bulge in her right cheek and said, "What hunt?"

Cooper was so proud of her that he got up, pulled her up and hugged her. He said, "There couldn't be a smarter or lovelier sister in the world."

Both Cali and Cooper went to boarding schools at an early age. Both looked forward to the holidays when they would be together again.

Cooper said, "When things are sad and hard for me, I go to the calendar and count how many days until I will see you again. This helps me a lot."

It was now 1860 and the war was on. Cooper was in his senior year in college, but was asked to take a commission in the army. He, of course, took it as he was fiercely patriotic. He looked so dashing in his uniform. It was a sad time for Cali, and she cried.

Cooper said, "Don't be sad for me. I will return, and we will have a lifetime together."

Just two months later during the first battle, Cooper was killed. His commanding officer wrote her and said, "I am so sorry. Lieutenant Cooper was hit in a cannon barrage, and there was nothing left of him. He was a good soldier."

Cali was devastated. Cooper was her life. She went on through college. She had some relationships, but no deep ones. When she was twenty-one her father took her to a ball. A client of his had become a good friend. His name was Robert Bridger. He had a son, Max, who was four years older than Cali. He had never married. This was mostly due to his life style. He just used women. He liked a variety, and seldom stayed with a woman very long after he had seduced her. It was the conquest that mattered to him.

He was introduced to Cali. She was a beauty. Max knew of the wealth of Cali's father, and also knew she was the only heir. He thought this could be a stepping stone to his success, even though his own father was wealthy.

He wooed Cali, but could tell immediately he could never seduce her. He decided to marry her and spoke often of marriage.

Even though Cali didn't particularly love him, she thought that he was the best catch she would ever see, so she consented to their marriage. It wasn't six months before they were sleeping in separate bedrooms.

As Max's father's business required him to move to Houston, Max and Cali moved, also. Max worked with his father a short time, but it was very boring to him. It also put a cramp in his carousing at night.

A state senator had retired and Max decided to run for his seat. Max was handsome and had a glib tongue. With his father's wealth, this brought him a victory.

Not two years later, he ran for congress, and that too was a success. He was sent to Washington DC. He rarely took Cali, as when he went, she went on to see her family in Boston. This gave him a time to take up his old hobby as a womanizer. Just a year later they were at a ball in Houston.

***

Cali looked across the room as her husband droned on. There she saw a handsome man who had Cooper's eyes. He looked at her just as Cooper had done with a piercing look. The thought of Cooper brought a rush of love over her. She was spellbound.. She had to know this man. She just pushed her way through the crowd around Max, never letting her eyes turn. Without dropping her eyes she said, "I'm Cali Bridger. That is my husband lecturing to some of his fans."

Kelly said, "I'm Kelly Andrews. Won't your husband be offended by me talking to his wife?"

"No, I think he is in love with his own voice, and is compelled to let his followers be dazzled by it."

"Would you like a drink, Mrs… …. Cali said, "Bridger, Cali Bridger. Yes, something that is fruity." The bartender had heard her and said, "Coming right up Mrs. Bridger."

She looked back at Kelly and said, "It's Cali to you. I can't get over how I am attracted to you. This has never happened to me in my life. Do you feel it like I do?"

Kelly did feel it, but said, "I think you are beautiful, but you're married."

"When a feeling comes on this strong, marriage has nothing to do with it."

119

"I think it does," said Kelly. "I'm attracted to you, but I also value the institution of marriage."

She now had her drink, and could see how uncomfortable Kelly was. She said, "We will meet again, it's destiny. You will see." She then put down her drink, and put both her arm around his neck, kissed him, then moved away.

Winston had concluded his meeting, and had turned around just in time to see Cali Bridger put her arm around Kelly's neck and kiss him. It was just a peck, but the kiss was on his lips.

Winston walked up and said, "I guess you know Mrs. Bridger. Where did you meet her?"

"I've never laid eyes on her before five minutes ago. Our eyes met, and she just walked towards me, never letting her eyes stray. She said that she was very attracted me. She told me she was married to Congressman Bridger, but that marriage had nothing to do with the attraction we had for one another. I was shocked. I told her although I was attracted to her, I also valued the institution of marriage. She told me we would meet again, as it was destiny. She then put her arm around me and kissed me. What do you make of this, Winston?"

"My gosh, I've seen her many times at functions like this, because her husband is a congressman. She never says a word, and seemed to be as cold as a fish. You are something, Kelly. Romanced by the belle of the ball. That could be dangerous."

"I was thinking that very thing. She told me that we would meet again, as it was destiny. It may be destiny for me to get shot," and Winston laughed.

He then said, "Were you smitten?"

"I have to admit, I was. No one has ever affected me like that woman. I want to go now."

Winston said, "Yes, I can't wait to tell Sara about his. She will be very interested. You see we must live our lives vicariously, now."

"I would like Sara's opinion. She may have better insight than the two of us."

"Yes, I think she will."

When they arrived, Winston made them a nightcap of sherry, and brought Sara a glass. She said, "Tell me all about the ball. Did you enjoy yourself, Kelly?"

"I had a strange thing happened to me that was a new experience. While Winston was engaged talking to three of his colleagues, I slipped away to the bar. I turned around to look at the crowd and I saw a man, well, not just a man, as I learned he was Congressman Bridger. He was talking to a the group around him.

"I looked just to his right, and saw his wife. Our eyes met, and I could not look away. I wanted to, but she kept looking at me. We stared at one another for another moment or so, then she walked straight for me, just pushing her way through the crowd, but never taking her eyes from me. I was terrified. I thought I might have met her somewhere, but then I would have remembered.

"When she arrived she said, 'Do you feel it?' I did, but denied it somewhat, but she said, 'I can't believe I am so attracted to you,' and asked if I felt the same. I told her I did, but that I also noticed that she was married. She said, 'That didn't matter.' I said, 'It mattered to me, because I believed in the sanctity of marriage.' She then said, 'We will meet again, it's destiny.' She then put her arm around my neck and kissed me on the lips and left."

"I would now like your opinion on what transpired."

Both Winston and Kelly leaned forward eagerly awaiting the female prospective."

She said, "That is delightfully fascinating. I have heard of these kind of things happening. I have read about them, but never experienced anything like that. Maybe it is destiny. I have also heard of people who can perceive the future. Maybe she does. How do you feel now."

"Scared. I want to run away. It's an eerie feeling like I can't get away from it. She beguiled me, like I've heard that witches could do."

"I can see that. You are to the point of shaking."

Kelly lifted his hand, and he was shaking. Winston got up and brought over a snifter of brandy and said, "You need a stronger drink tonight. I think you should stay here with us tonight. We will talk, and maybe that feeling will leave you."

Sara turned to Winston and said, "Kelly has brought some excitement to our lives, Winston. I can't wait to see how this plays out."

Kelly said, "Please, let's talk about something else, my nerves are frazzled."

Winston brought up the coming elections, and what they would mean for Houston. Sara said, "Winston, there must be something else to talk about, other than that dumb election"

Winston grinned at Kelly and said, "Nothing can top what happened tonight. I'm like Sara, I can't wait to see how this plays out."

Kelly didn't spend the night. He went back to his hotel room. He decided to leave and go to New York City. He needed to see about investing his money, rather than letting it sit in a bank drawing little interest. He also wanted out of Houston, where he might just run into Cali Bridger or her husband.

Winston saw him off on a ship. He was booked in first class, and had an excellent cabin. He had boarded at night after dinner, and went straight to his cabin, and went to bed. He rose early the next morning and stepped out. He breathed in the fresh salt air that invigorated him. He decided to take a walk around the deck. He had only walked a few steps when Cali Bridges joined him. He was flabbergasted.

She said, "I told you it was destiny. Neither of us knew the other was going to be on this ship, but here we are."

They walked over to the railing away from others, and Kelly said, "I guess you were right. Do you see other things in the future?

"No, but I knew I was right about this. I had a feeling the minute I saw you, that you were in my future. I don't know why or how, but I knew. You have the eyes of my brother, who I loved more than anyone in the world. Once I saw your eyes I knew."

"Where is your brother now?"

"He was taken in the war, and I'm still not over it yet. However, I expect you to take his place."

"As a brother?"

"No, silly, as the most important person in my life. My husband and I quit sleeping together six months after we were married. He's a womanizer. It's just part of his make up. I found out, and it ended there with me. I then knew he loves only himself, and just uses women. I just thought this was the way it would be the rest of my life. Then I saw you. I knew immediately that we were destined to be together."

Kelly asked, "Where are you headed?"

I'm going to Boston where my folks live. My aunt is very sick. She loves me dearly as I do her, so I'm going there. Where are you headed?"

"I'm going to New York City. I have accumulated some wealth, and am going to try and learn how to manipulate it, as it is only drawing very low interest. I plan to educate myself, so that I can make wise investments."

"My father is a broker and I love that business. When we are married, we can do that together."

"You must get a divorce before we can be seen together. How do you plan to do that?"

"My husband has a manager who plots most of his actions. He hates me, and I him. I'll go to him, and tell him I'm going to divorce Max. He'll handle everything so it won't hurt Max's career. It will take some time, but by this time next year, I will be single."

"Meanwhile, what?"

"Meanwhile we can see each other in New York City. I know a hotel not far from where our ship will dock, that will be a good place. It's swanky enough for good taste, but not overly so. People of our class won't stay there, because of its proximity to the waterfront. I've stayed there many times as it's handy. Its name is the Metropolitan. We can stay there when we dock."

"Your not suggesting that we stay together are you?"

"No, I know how prudish you are. Have you ever been with a woman?"

"What kind of a question is that? Don't you think that is a little too personal?"

"I suppose so, but I want to know everything about you in the next few months. Where is your cabin?"

"On this deck, cabin twenty. I'll meet you for lunch at the lounge on this deck. I need to change."

They parted and Kelly thought, *"What have I gotten myself into. I know we will marry as she beguiled me. I think about her constantly."*

They met for lunch and both gave short descriptions of their lives. They took all their meals together, but never went to each others cabin. By the time they docked, they knew each other quite well. Both were in love.

14

NEW YORK CITY

Cali took Kelly to the Metropolitan. He checked in, then took her to Union Station to catch the train to Boston. They kissed goodbye and she was gone.

Kelly went to Wall street. He decided to go to the stock exchange to see what he could learn. He was excited by what he saw. He met a man about his age who seemed to be trading very rapidly. His name was Sam Vern. As Sam was extremely busy, Kelly asked, "Could I buy you a drink when the day is over?"

"Sure," Sam replied. I'll meet you at that door.," and pointed.

When they were in a pub, Sam ordered a pint of ale. Kelly did the same. Sam said, "So what's on your mind?"

"I've accumulated a small amount of money, and want to invest it. I need someone to teach me the ropes."

"I'm just a runner, and really don't know much about trading. I want to learn, too. I heard of a class that's starting next week. It only cost twenty dollars for a semester. The guy teaching the class is a master at investing. He's made a fortune in the market. His name is Lenard Coy. I think the reason he teaches the class is because he likes it so much he wants to teach other how to invest.

They enrolled and Kelly was engrossed in Coy's message. Coy began with the history of the market and then went into what makes a stock great or not so great. He told of the tools available to them to investigate each stock.

Kelly took notes, then visited brokerages to utilize the tools that Coy spoke about. At one of the Brokerages, Kelly ran into Coy. They talked about two stocks that Coy was hot on.

It was lunch time and Kelly asked Coy if he could treat him to lunch. Coy agreed and took him to a place down an alley and over a block. It was a mom and pop café.

Coy said, "Not too many people know about this place and I'm glad. Once a person eats their cuisine, they are hooked. Don't tell anyone about this place or it will become popular and the food will become worse." This made Kelly smile.

Coy then began talking about the twos stocks he thought were great. He pointed out there qualities then the dangers that might occur. Kelly was fascinated with Coy's insight.

Kelly asked, "Are you going to invest in them?"

"Yes, I see their upside has great potential."

Kelly asked, "How does one invest?"

"At present you must do this through a broker. I have a friend who charges me much less in brokerage fee as I trade a lot and he handles it personally." "I think I'll invest in those two stocks. Will you introduce me to your broker?"

"I would be happy to. How much do you plan to invest?"

"Just a little to start, maybe five thousand on each."

"My lord, you must be a rich man?"

"I have accumulated a modest sum, and want to put it to work for me, as you put it in your lecture last night. I find your lectures the most interesting of anything I have ever encountered. I'm as hooked on investing as you are. Will you tell me when you are selling what you buy?"

"Sure, I like to talk over my investments. It makes me think better."

Coy's broker was genially glad to meet Kelly, and because he was investing ten thousand dollars, he gave Kelly the same discount as he did Coy.

They began meeting at lunch everyday and talked over every investment. Kelly began investing in the stocks that Coy owned.

***

Cali came for the weekend. She had written him a postcard telling her estimated time of arrival and what train she was on. Kelly was at Union station. They kissed and Kelly took her bags. He had already rented a hack and he was waiting for them at the entrance of the station.

Kelly had acquired the room next to his. She brought him up to date on what had transpired with her aunt. Kelly told her about his class on investing.

Cali said, "I wish I could attend those classes with you. I can see how enthused you are, and I would be just as enthused. I see our marriage will be filled with trading and the excitement it brings. My father is so wrapped up in it that we seldom see him."

"Yes, it will be a great hobby if not a vocation. There is endless research which I find fun to do. I spend most of my day at a brokerage firm looking up the history of stocks. I have a friend who does this with me, Lenard Coy. He's the one who teaches the class I attend. He knows more about the market than anyone. He's spent his entire life trading. He told me that is why he never married. He says if women traded, he's sure he would be married. However, I've never seen a woman in any of the places of trade."

"When we're married, they will start seeing one. I can't wait. I see this binding us together."

"I hope so, because I love it."

Cali then told how she had decided to live at home for awhile then start spending more time in New York City. She said, "I will have to go to Houston to get that albatross from around my neck. Both Max and his manager will probably be elated over losing me. "I think I should go next week and get the process started. What do you think?"

"I have no insight on divorces, so just do what you think best."

Cali left on a Monday and said, "I may not see you for a few months, but when I do, I hope to have some good news for you."

When she arrived in Houston, she went straight to Barry Hanson's office. He was surprised to see her.

Cali said, "Mr. Hanson it's easy to see you don't like me as you see me as a stumbling block to Max's career. I think that Max and I should divorce. Can you make that happen?"

Again Hanson was shocked, but didn't show it. He took a moment to digest what she had just told him then said, "I think I can. Do you want anything from Max?"

"No, just the divorce. I have my own legacy that will keep me quite comfortable. I don't want to hurt Max or his career. I think he will be happy to be free of me, as our marriage was over long ago. I just want to be free again and maybe find someone who I can love, if that is possible."

Hanson said, "You have been candid with me and I thank you for that. I, too, think that it will be better for you both. I now have to think how to handle this so that Max's career will not suffer. It may take some time. Are you going back to live with your folks?"

"Yes, but I will be available when needed. I don't want Max's career hurt because of this, so I will show up when I'm needed."

"You are a good woman, Cali, and I'll do my best to make you and Max happy."

After Cali left, Hanson went to see Robert Bridger. He related all that transpired. After listening to Hanson, he said, "I wish we could just make her disappear. I see a divorce as very messy. Even if we do our best to keep it out of the press, some paper will pick up on it and then it will be a hot news item."

"What are you suggesting, Robert?"

"Only that she disappears. I don't want to know the details. Just handle it."

Hanson got Robert's message. He had met several of the sea captains Robert employed. He had heard a rumor that a Captain Cruz trafficked in white women who he delivered to plantation owners and brothels in the Caribbean islands and South America. He decided to meet with this captain.

He went to the harbor master and asked him if the *Simon Bolivar* would be putting in to Houston in the near future. He was told he wouldn't be, but that he was scheduled to be in New York City the next month.

Hanson decided to write Cali and tell her that in the coming month he would like her to come to New York City to sign some papers for her divorce. He later received the news when Captain Cruz would be in New York.

Hanson was at the docks when the *Simon Bolivar* docked. He came aboard and met with Captain Cruz. Hanson told about Cali and how he would like to dispose of her. He told of her beauty and young age.

Captain Cruz was interested. He asked, Does she stay in New York City at times?

Yes, I am told she stays at the Metropolitan Hotel near the dock."

"Is she alone when she stays there?"

"Yes."

"I think we can do business. I'll give you five hundred dollars. I would give you more if you delivered her to me the night of my sailing, but there is expenses if I have to extract her from the hotel."

"I understand. I will add, if you just drop her off at sea, I will not care."

"Now that will cost you five-hundred. If you agree, we will just say I will take her off your hands with no exchange of cash."

"A good exchange. If you will give me a time, when you return to New York, I will have your lady at the Metropolitan."

"That will be in two weeks. I'm making a run down the St. Lawrence River and will be back the twenty-sixth. You can then give me her room number. I will have my men pick her up the night of the twenty-seventy as we sail that night."

Hanson left and immediately wrote Cali that she needed to sign the divorce papers the twenty-seventh. He added he would have to know her room number.

In the meantime, Kelly had found an apartment he could buy that was near the stock exchange. Coy lived in the same building and put him on to it.

He wrote Cali his new address.

Cali wrote Hanson that she would be in New York City the twenty-seventh and would be staying at the Metropolitan in room 207. She had received a letter from Kelly telling about his new apartment. She said she may have some good news for him, and would meet him the evening of the twenty-eighth.

CHAPTER 15

THE ABDUCTION

Hanson met her at her room the twenty-seventh. He had papers for her to sign. She asked how long it would be until the divorce was final. He told her about a month. She went to bed early as she wanted to surprise Kelly by knocking on his door early the next day.

Around eleven o'clock that night Cali heard a knock on her door. She got up and said, "Who is it?"

One of the sailors said, "It's a message from Mr. Hanson?"

She opened the door and was immediately taken by a huge man with a hand over her mouth. He said, "If you will be quiet, we will not harm you. If you yell, we will just cut your throat and leave. Which will it be?"

He took his hand off her mouth and she said, "I'll be quiet. Where are you taking me?"

"To a ship."

"May I get dressed?" The man nodded and she put on some pants and a warm blouse. While she was dressing she heard one of the men say, "Captain Cruz said we must be back before twelve."

Cali said, "I need to use the bathroom."

One of the men looked to see if there was another entrance and there wasn't so she was permitted to go in. She immediately took her cuticle scissors and stood on the commode and carved over the door, "Captain Cruz," in small letters. She then flushed the commode. Before going out, she put her cuticle scissors and a few other personal items she would need to groom herself in her pockets, and opened the door.

She was taken to the ship and they left with the tide at twelve that night.

Kelly went to the Metropolitan the twenty-eighth and went to her room. He knocked, but of course there was no answer. He went to the lobby and waited until seven p. m. thinking she may have gone shopping. However after seven he knew she would be back by then. He went to the clerk again to make sure she had checked in, and was assured she had.

Kelly was in a quandary. He sat and thought. He asked the clerk to take him up to examine her room. He explained that he had an appointment with her. The clerk let him in and stood by while he examined the room. He was about to leave when he thought of the clue that Cooper had left her about the agate. He went into the bathroom and could see something had been scratched about the sill of the door. He stood on his tiptoes and could see the name, "Captain Cruz," had been scratched. He then knew she had been abducted. He decided to consult with his boss, Colonel Alfred. Before he left he went by the harbormaster's office and learned that Captain Cruz commanded the *Simon Bolivar*. It was headed for Cuba, some of the islands and eventually to Buenos Aries. That left him no clue to where Cali was other than south of Florida. He then left for Washington DC.

Alfred said, "Being she is a Congressman's wife, this has federal implications. I'll see the attorney general tomorrow and discuss it with him. Kelly went with Alfred, but didn't go to the meeting with the attorney general, but waited outside his office.

After less than a half hour, Alfred appeared and said, "The A. G. wants you on the case immediately. We will keep it silent, as several people could be implicated.

As they were traveling, Kelly said, "She has a bad relationship with Congressman Bridger's chief of staff. She also is at odds with her husband and his father. Any or all of them could be responsible for her abduction."

Alfred asked, "What is your relationship with Mrs. Bridger?" I am just a friend. I had an appointment with her to discuss some investments, and she failed to show up, so I went to her room to investigate."

He then told of finding the name of Captain Cruz scratched over the door sill. He added what he learned from the harbormaster.

Alfred said, "Well at least you have a start. The attorney general said that he would approve two thousand dollars to find Mrs. Bridger."

"I will need some help on this one. I see going to South America, and I don't speak Spanish. I would like Lenard Valdez to help me."

"A good choice, Kelly. He owes you one."

Kelly knew that Valdez lived just outside Washington DC, so he went to his house.

Lenard invited him in and introduced him to his wife, Maria. Kelly then told them the entire story, leaving out only his personal involvement with Cali. After hearing Kelly, Lenard said, "I see this as requiring more than just us. I want to take Maria, as she once lived in Cuba. I think Cruz might have taken her there. I also, have a brother, Ruben, who works with the treasury department. He is gifted in the arts, and I see him valuable in getting Mrs. Bridger back. What about her husband?"

"He may be involved, so we shouldn't contact him or his office or father. They may all be involved."

The next day they went back to see Colonel Alfred to get the funds for Lenard, his wife and Ruben. Alfred agreed that all were needed.

Alfred said, "We had a similar case to this about ten years ago. We used a cover story to keep anyone from knowing about the abduction. We said the guy had tuberculosis, and had been sent to a sanitarium in Colorado. We said that his disease was contagious, so correspondence would have to come through the government. It worked out well. I suggest that a similar letter go out to Mrs. Bridger's family and to the Bridger's family. I'll take care of that end.

Kelly said, "We need to find the *Simon Bolivar*. If Mrs. Bridger was aboard, I would bet she would leave another clue in her cabin."

***

Cali was now in a cabin next to the captain's quarters. She knew that if Kelly was smart enough to get her first clue, she would have to leave him another clue as to where she would be taken off the ship. She knew if she put down how long she was aboard, he could figure out where she debarked from the ship.

She marked over her hatch, days and hours. Each day she would scratch a mark. It took three days and a half to reach Havana, Cuba. She could hear them docking and she marked the third day and scratched in ½.

She was taken to a carriage, and they traveled about three hours out of Havana. They arrived at an estate that was walled in by a twelve foot high stone wall. It had towers at all four corners. A wrought-iron gate had a guard that let them in. They went to the manor house and a man said, "Wait here." He left and about ten minutes later a nice looking man came out, and had her get out of the carriage. He had her turn around and then said, "Si," and paid the man a lot of money.

A woman appeared and said something in Spanish that Cali understood to mean, "Follow me," so she followed the woman. The woman soon found that Cali spoke no Spanish, so she spoke in English to her.

She said, "My name is Nina. If you will do everything I tell say, you may last a few months or more. If you do not comply, you will be sent to a brothel. There you may live a couple of years, but with the diseases and all, not many make if past two years.

Cali thought, *"Maybe I would have a better chance of escape from a brothel,"* but then thought better of it, because if Senor Esteban knew her husband was a United States Congressman, she would probably just be killed.

Cali said, "I haven't eaten all day, may I have something to eat?"

"Yes, I have some fruit in my room. I'll get some for you. Right now I will take you to your room. You will be rooming with a Chinese woman named, Chin. She speaks English, so she will acquaint you with what will be expected of you.

Chin was a pretty woman just over five feet in height. She had a nice smile and said, "Welcome. I hope we will be friends."

Cali said, "Under the circumstances I need all the friends I can get. Were you taken here against your will."

"Of course, all of us were. However, the two Spanish women like it here. They evidently lived in poverty, and this is a step up for them. I'm from California, and was kidnapped. Although I would rather be home, this is my circumstance and I'm learning to adjust to it."

"What will I be expected to do?"

"Sleep with Estabon when he desires you. That will probably be about once a week, as I think he likes the two Spanish girls to me, as they do special things to him. I will warn you to try and please Estabon as best you can, for if he tires of you, you may be sent to a brothel on one of the islands. I have no proof of this. It's just what Nina told me.

"Estabon entertains on the weekends, so sometimes you may have to sleep with one of his guests. I have had to once. My advice is to just play along, and see what happens. We are required to exercise everyday. In the morning we go for a run, then exercise, and go for a swim. Sometimes, Estabon swims with us, but not too often. We go nude as that is what Estabon wants.

"In the afternoons we sometimes go riding. However, this is supervised by two men who ride with us. They are both armed. Nina told us that if we try to run away, they have orders to shoot us. We also have archery and other games in the afternoon.

"They feed us well, but only small portions. Apparently, Estabon doesn't want us to gain weight. We have cocktails everyday at five o'clock. You can have two drinks of your choice. They serve fruit juice with rum. It's very good."

"Are you working on a plan to get away?"

"That would be practically impossible. Estabon has guards that are watchful. If you were to escape, where would you go. You don't know the geography and don't speak the language. Unless you have outside help, it's hopeless.

"No one knows where you are or where to look, so you see it's hopeless. I suggest that you do like me and make the best of what it is."

Nina did bring Cali some fruit, which she shared with Chin, as Cali realized you were hungry most of the time due to the small portions of food. Nina brought Cali some clothes. The dresses were risqué. She had silk underwear and stockings. The shoes that were brought were a bit big, but not so as she could not wear them. In all the clothes were nice, just a bit suggestive. She had two evening dress. Chin told her that she was required to wear them at the evening meal.

The cocktails were good. When they were called to dinner, the girls all stood until Estabon had taken his seat. The meal was excellent, but about half what Cali generally ate. She thought to herself, *"I can get used to this. It's probably healthier than what I generally eat."*

When they were in their room, Nina came by and said, "He wants you tonight, Cali. Try to please him the best you can. It's for your own good."

Nina helped pick out what Cali was to wear. Nina took her to Estabon's room.

Nina said, "Sit on that chair until Estabon comes. When he enters the room, rise and walk into his arms with a smile."

Esteban entered the room, and had a robe on. He said, "I need a bath, please draw one for me and bathe me."

Cali complied. The bathtub was the largest she had ever seen. As she drew the bath she saw some bath salts, and put them in the tub. They made a foam.

Esteban came in and removed his robe. He said, "Bathe with me." So Cali removed her night clothes, and stepped into the tub with him. He washed himself, then turned his back and said, "Scrub my back," which she did.

They then dried. Esteban said, "Don't bother with the night clothes, I like to sleep nude. They went to the bed, and Esteban made love to her. They didn't do anything out of the ordinary. The next morning he made love to her again.

Cali learned that just like Chin had said, he used two of the girls much more often than he did Cali, and Chin.

***

Kelly learned that the *Simon Bolivar,* was due back in New York harbor in two months from when it left. They just had to wait. Lenard and Marie went home and Kelly said he would notify them when Cruz was to return.

The only thing Kelly could do was to go back to trading. He did check each day with the harbormaster on the return of Cruz's ship.

He finally got the word that Cruz would be docking that week. The hour it docked, Kelly was at the pier. He waited until the unloading was completed. It was then the middle of the afternoon. Kelly could see the officer of the deck was on duty at the gangplank alone.

Kelly approached the officer and said, "I have been paid to look at the cabin a beautiful woman used when she was aboard your ship. She left a picture there that she thinks is still in her cabin. I'll give you fifty dollars if you will permit me to search her cabin.

The officer looked both ways then said, "I'll give you about three minutes to search, before I call the master-at-arms."

"Time enough," Kelly said, and handed him a fifty dollar note.

Once in the cabin, Kelly shut the hatch. He pulled a chair over and stood looking over the sill. Above the seal was scratched three marks and a half, then the word, "days."

Kelly was elated. He put the chair back, then came out and said, "It wasn't there," and left.

He didn't even go home. He went to Union Station and boarded a train to Washington DC. When he arrived he told Valdez what he had found.

Valdez said, "She's in Cuba. We need to go there, and locate the largest plantations around Havana. Maria and I will ask question about seeing a beautiful white lady. She would be remembered as not too many beautiful white women arrive there. If nothing turns up around Havana, we will then branch out. I think this may take some time.

I would like to take my brother, Ruben. He's good at these things. As I told you, he works at the treasury department. He can get leave as he has a vacation coming.

They left and went to Ruben's house. He didn't even question them. If a congressmen's wife was missing he would go.

They left for New York City the next morning. When they arrived, Kelly made arrangements for sailing to Havana. It was two more days before they could get accommodations.

When they arrived they took hotel rooms near the dock, and began asking question. They found that there were three large plantations near

Havana. No one could remember a white woman, but one man said, "I know the plantations have women for the owner's entertainment. One owner, Senor Estabon, is not married. He keeps several women of different races."

They decided to concentrate on Estabon's plantation. Lenard suggested that they find out what services Esteban's estate needed. This led them to an agency that Esteban used to secure his goods and personnel. Lenard approached the agency asking for a job. He had a written resume that he handed the manager and owner of the agency, a Roberto Languorous. Roberto was impressed and said, "There may be an opening soon. Tell me about your experience."

"I worked for the Pinkerton agency in New York City, and an agency in the Bahamas. I have letters of recommendation from both."

"That won't be necessary. I'll take your word for it. Give me your address and if something comes up, I'll let you know."

"One other thing Senor Languorous, I have a brother with the same qualities and I also has a wife, who is an experienced cook."

"That is good to know. Families should stay together. I have a large family, and I work to see that all my family stays near. I'll see what I can do."

Lenard said, "An estate the size of Senor Esteban's must use a lot of goods. Maybe I could get on with one of the suppliers, while I am waiting for a security job to open."

"That is showing some initiative, Senor Valdez. I will write a couple of their names and addresses for you. You may get a job driving a wagon until something turns up."

Lenard shared the news with Kelly, Maria and Ruben. They immediately approached a grocery supplier and he said, "If you have your own wagon I will employ you. Senor Esteban wants a load of liquor delivered.."

Lenard said, "Yes, we do have our own wagon. When will you want us?"

"Tomorrow at seven in the morning."

Lenard interrupted for Kelly what had transpired, and they went and bought a team and wagon. They were there at seven in the morning, and loaded four kegs of beer, three kegs of wine and many cases of whisky, rum and gin. They then headed for Esteban's estate.

When they arrived, the guards searched them for weapons, but they had concealed them in a drawer that pulled out from under the seat. A guard went with them to unload the liquor. Kelly could see women swimming, but they were at the far end of the estate.

Kelly said, "Offer him ten pesos if he will let us have a closer look at the girls."

Lenard made the offer while holding the pesos. The guard said, "What does it matter," and took the ten pesos. They went within twenty feet, behind a hedge. Kelly could see Cali. They watched for just a little while, then the guard pulled on their shirts and they left and unloaded the liquor.

The guard said, "Those are Senor Esteban's women. He takes turns sleeping with them. He uses them a year or so then sells them. I wish I had the money to buy one."

They left and started planning their assault.

CHAPTER 16

THE RESCUE OF CALI

They decided to wait a couple of weeks to see if Senor Languorous could put them in Esteban's estate as guards. A week later they checked in with Languorous and he said he had a slot for a cook. After some haggling over wages, Maria was hired. She was to be at the estate at seven in the morning, and worked until nine in the evening. The work was seven days a week.

She did not sleep there, so she was let out and picked up at the gate by Lenard. He had bought a two wheeled buggy, and used one of the horse that Kelly had bought. While Lenard was waiting in the evenings, he made friends with the gate guards.

Kelly knew he couldn't rush things, as to do so, may cost one of them their lives, and Cali would be stuck forever. A month and a half later, Languorous sent a message to them saying that two security guards were needed. As Maria had worked out fine, and she was the wife of Lenard, an interview with Esteban was made. They were hired.

A month later, another guard quit and Ruben and Lenard went to Esteban and told him they had a friend they had known for years, who was very good at security. Lenard said, "He speaks only English, but then most people here speak English, so I know he would work out."

Kelly was hired after Esteban interviewed him. Kelly had a prefabricated story of working for a detective agency, where he escorted three women and a man to Santa Fe from St. Louis. He told of Indian trouble and that he was able to hold off a small war party.

Kelly had a letter of recommendation from Languorous, so Esteban hired him. All three were put on the day shift as the older guards liked the night shift, because they slept most of the time.

The estate had two guard posts that were on top of the wall at opposite corners of the wall around the estate. There was a guard on each of these towers. They were served coffee at ten in the morning and at three in the afternoon. Maria volunteered for this duty.

There were four outside guards, and two inside guards. The inside guards were Esteban's bodyguards wherever he went.

Kelly said, "We can use knockout drops for the outside guard. You can put the knockout drops in the coffee for the outside guards, Maria, then you can bring coffee to the inside guards."

The outside guard brought his tin cup to be served, but didn't drink it until he was back at the gate. They set a date for Sunday, as there would be no deliveries, and it was generally quiet through the day.

At ten that morning, Maria served the coffee. Everyone went back to their posts. Ruben, Lenard and Kelly acted like they were drinking their coffee, but didn't. The guard were fast asleep within ten minutes. During that time Maria had served the inside guards coffee, also. When they dozed off, Maria came to the front with a cloth and waved it, showing that the inside guards were asleep.

Esteban and the girls were swimming. Near ten-thirty, they all came to the house to change for lunch. Chin had stayed at the pool with one of the other girls as they wanted to swim laps. They did this everyday, and Nina stayed with them.

When Cali entered her room, Kelly was sitting in a chair facing her door. He raised his finger to his mouth indicating for her to be silent. She closed the door and raced into his arms.

Kelly said, "We have only an hour to make our escape. All the guards were given knockout drops with their coffee. They will be asleep for some four hours. We must be in Havana by then, as we have passage on a ship bound for New York City at three. Pack what you need. I will be talking to Esteban. Now get to your task."

Kelly left and went into Esteban's office where he was working. He turned and said, "What are you doing in the house?"

"I have come to recover a United States Congressman's wife. She is Mrs. Max Bridger from the state of Texas. I will not arrest you as we are in a foreign country, but if you ever set foot in America again, you will be prosecuted for kidnapping.

"I would suggest that you give the other girls free passage to where they are from. The president of the United States will be sending a letter to the King of Spain detailing your activities here in Cuba. You might want to relocate."

Kelly could see Esteban's hand opening a drawer. Kelly pulled his derringer and said, "If you try to resist, I will not kill you, but I will shoot you in both knees, so you will be a cripple the rest of your life, so close that drawer."

Esteban complied. Kelly said, "Get up and go into the parlor." When they arrived Cali was there and Kelly asked, "Do you want me to kill him or cripple him?"

Cali said, "No, I wasn't hurt other than having to bed him once a week. However, he needs to learn a lesson. Maybe we should remove his penis, so he doesn't trifle with other women."

Kelly said, "We don't have that much time. The authorities will come down on him and maybe put him in a Spanish prison. Once in there, the only way out is death."

They then left. They had a carriage and all five of them traveled to Havana. They were there just in time to catch the ship.

As they were sailing away, Cali said, "I thought you would be able to follow the clues I left, but I wasn't sure. I had made up my mind to stay a year before I planned an escape. I had great faith in your ability."

Kelly said, "You had more faith than I did. I thought I had lost you forever."

When they arrived in New York City, Kelly gave both brothers an extra five hundred dollars for their help. They both tried to refuse it, but Kelly insisted.

Kelly said, "I may need your help in arresting Captain Cruz. We need to put him out of business and in prison."

Aboard the ship home, they discussed what to do about Captain Cruz, and whoever had bribed him. They decided to go to Washington DC and get Colonel Alfred's opinion.

After hearing what had transpired in Cuba, Alfred said, "I'll have to discuss this with the attorney general. I will see him tomorrow."

They took a hotel rooms in Langley. The third day they were summoned to Colonel Alfred's office. He said, "The attorney general is writing the king of Spain about Senor Esteban, and what happened in Cuba. I think that will put Esteban out of business. He is probably in another country by now.

"The attorney general thought you should have the pleasure of arresting Captain Cruz. He said that several soldiers would accompany you to the docks when Captain Cruz arrives. You will take him to Washington DC, where he will be interrogated and given a lighter sentence if he discloses who set this up."

Cali said, "I know who set this up. It was Barry Hansen. It may even include Robert Bridger. I don't think my husband is involved, but you never know."

Colonel Alfred said, "Well, we will know soon enough."

They knew approximately when the *Simon Bolivar* would arrive. They waited with a squad of soldiers. When the ship docked, a gangplank was put out from the ship to the dock. As sailors scramble to tie up the ship, Kelly, Lenard and Cali went aboard. The officer of the deck saw that both men had their badges out, and were carrying pistols in the other hand.

What Kelly didn't know was that Captain Cruz had set up a drill that all hands had practiced. If authorities tried to come aboard, every man was to do something. The deckhands were to untie the ship, the gangplank was to be removed and the ship immediately started to back out until they could turn around. The master-at-arms had riflemen, who would defend the ship until the people, who were trying to arrest them, were either all dead or had surrendered.

The officer of the deck immediately blew his whistle three times, and every sailor went to his duty. He said nothing to Kelly or Lenard, but blew a shrill whistle three times then paused and blew it again.

Immediately the sailors untied the ropes, and the gangplank was lifted as the ship backed away from the dock. Lenard pointed his gun at the officer of the deck and said, "Stop this or I will shoot you dead."

The officer of the deck said, "I can't stop this. Only the captain has that authority."

"Take us to the engine room. If you do anything out of the ordinary, I have the authority to kill you." They were off, and went down a ladder, then another ladder. They were now all in the bowels of the ship.

Kelly could hear the engines, and motioned with his gun for the officer to lead on to the engine room. When they arrived, the hatch leading to the engine room, was locked.

Kelly then motioned for the officer to go back. They reached the main deck and could see several sailors with rifles.

Kelly said, "If you don't lower your weapons, then you will be charged as an accessory to kidnapping a federal officer, You can never set foot in America again." Two lowered their rifles, but several didn't.

Kelly shouted to take cover, and they all dived for some piles of ropes. Kelly stood his ground, and killed two of the men who had rifles. They fired, but missed Kelly.

Kelly yelled, "Lenard take Cali, and go overboard. We're not that far from shore."

Lenard reacted immediately. He pulled Cali to the edge of the ship, and threw her overboard. Then he jumped."

Kelly shot toward another man with a rifle and winged him. He then raced to the ships railing, and dived over. He never let go of his pistol. He hit the water feet first. When he surfaced, he could see two riflemen shooting at him. Both missed. Kelly shot at them and his bullet hit the railing between the two riflemen, and they both pulled back.

The ship pulled away, and was now turning around. It then went down the river to open waters. As Kelly swam toward the docks he thought, *"I should have taken the soldiers aboard first."*

Cali and Lenard had made it to shore. Cali had hit the water awkwardly, and lost her breath. Lenard swam toward her and pulled her to shore. All three were on the dock now, but were smarting from what just happened.

Kelly said, "How dumb of me not to have anticipated that. If we ever do that again, the soldiers will go aboard first and there will be no fighting. I guess I was just too anxious to arrest Cruz."

When they returned to Langley, Colonel Alfred said, "It could have happened to anyone, Kelly. Don't blame yourself. I'll notify the Navy that an act of war has been made against a federal officer by the *Simon Bolivar*. They will handle it."

"No one knows where Cruz is going," Kelly expounded.

Lenard said, "He only knows the islands and South America. Spain controls most of that. I will report to the attorney general, and he will suggest that the king be notified at once of Captain Cruz's actions."

CHAPTER 17

FINDING HEAVEN

Kelly sat with Cali, and they tried to think of how best to find Captain Cruz. They first thought of the U. S. Navy, but were told by Colonel Alfred that the navy had been downsized after the war, and had a very small budget. The navy now had just enough to pay for a very small number of men and maintain a few ships. They then realized that it would be up to them, if justice were to be served on Captain Cruz.

Having no clue of how they would find the *Simon Bolivar* and Captain Cruz, they decided to go see Leland and Linda. They knew nothing about Cali, and Cali knew very little about Leland and Linda.

When taking a buckboard from Kansas City, they had plenty of time for Kelly to tell her all he knew about them.

Cali said, "You mean Leland took a saloon girl to live with?"

"Cali, all of us end up doing the things we do through circumstances, sometimes beyond our control. Linda may have made some bad choices along the way, but maybe circumstances pushed her into that trade. I'm surely not one to judge her. Compared to me, she's a saint. I have taken as many lives, as she has slept with men. I'm sure God judges that much more harshly than lying with man."

"You're right. I slept with Esteban many times. I just did what I had to do. Linda probably just did what she had to do. The main thing about her living with Leland is that they did it for a good purpose. If they love each other, then I'm sure God blesses their union."

"I know Leland needed her as much as she needed Leland. It's not good to live alone. I had a lot of that, but God compensated me by loaning me two good women."

"That's a strange way to put it, Kelly"

"Well, we are only on this earth for a short period, and we don't choose our time of being born, or when we die. Most people are surprised when their time comes, but some are taken suddenly, and they have no idea."

"Do you ever think about the hereafter, Kelly?"

"I suppose most people think about it from time to time. I have had very little to do with religion. I know there is a heaven and a hell. I also know there is a God, and he had a son named Jesus, who came to earth to save men. I really don't know too much about that. When I was in the war a young man tried to tell me about Jesus, but there wasn't time for me to understand it all. He was killed the next day and I felt God took him to heaven. Do you know much about it?"

"Yes. My mother was religious, and I went with her to Sunday school and church every Sunday. My father would never go. Mother told me he was afraid to go. I never understood that. However, I was taught that only by blood can sins be forgiven. It says so in the Bible, I'm told.

"The Jews killed animals, as God instructed them to do, to cover their sins. But this was just a temporary fix, and they had to do it ever so often. When Moses asked the king of Egypt for permission to leave, it made the king of Egypt mad. Moses asked several times and each time the king refused. A terrible curse came upon Egypt.

"Moses came to the king the last time, and asked that the Jews be released. It made the king so mad he decided to have the eldest child of each

Jewish family killed. However, before this could be carried out, God came to Moses, and told him that his people were to kill a lamb, and put the blood above their doors and to each side because an angel would come that night, and slay the eldest child whose door didn't have the blood on the door.

"The Jews did this, and each child was spared where the blood was, but every Egyptian's eldest child was slain, even the son of the king.

"The king then knew he must let the Jews go. That in called the *Passover*, and the Jews celebrate that event every year. I didn't tell it exactly like it really happened, but you get the idea."

"Yes, I've heard of the *Passover*, but had no idea what it meant."

"When God sent Jesus to the earth in the form of a man, He knew that Jesus must be sacrificed, and His blood would cover the sins of all people who received Jesus as their Savior."

"Have you received him, Cali?"

"Yes, as a ten year old, I remembering asking Jesus to come into my heart. I have not been to church for some time now. I know I must do that, do you want to go with me?"

"Yes. Everything we do, we will do together. Let's talk to Leland and Linda about it when we arrive, as I know Leland loves philosophy. He will at least like to talk about it."

When they arrived Leland was really glad to see them. The way he hugged Kelly, it filled Cali's heart with love. Linda was very quiet, and didn't say much as she realized that Cali was a lady.

After the introductions, Linda said, "Would you like to freshen up Mrs. Bridger?"

"Just Cali, Linda." As they went to a room that had a basin Cali said, "I feel you are uncomfortable with me, so let me put you at ease. I was kidnapped, and lived on a plantation in Cuba. I slept with a man there and did things that you had to do with men, so you see we are both in the same boat.

"I'm married to a man who doesn't love me, and sleeps with other women. I plan to divorce him, and marry Kelly. So don't feel uneasy around me."

Linda said, "Thank you so much. You have helped me a lot."

Cali said, "I feel the four of us should talk this all out. None of us know when God will take us, and we need to get ready for that. Do you believe in God?"

"Yes, I pray all the time, but don't know much about God as I have never read a Bible. None of the girls I worked with ever discussed it, because we all knew we were sinning."

"Would it be alright if I brought the subject up? Kelly and I discussed it a lot coming here. Kelly doesn't know much either. He said a young man was telling him about Jesus, but they had to go into battle, and never got to finish their conversation, because the man was killed that day. Kelly said he felt good about the man, as he knew he was in heaven with Jesus. So, I know Kelly will want to talk about it."

"I think Leland will too. He loves to talk about things like this. He's such a deep person. I thank the Lord each night for letting me have him. What are the odds of a respected rancher taking in a saloon girl?"

That night after dinner, they were sitting around and Cali said, "I would like to talk about heaven and hell. I want to go to heaven, and I would really like all of us to go there."

Leland said, "That is a mighty deep subject, the kind I love to explore. Living on the ranch some ten miles from town, we rarely went to church. However, I learned about the love of Jesus as did Patty and her mother. We all were baptized, so I know they are in heaven. I feel inadequate to say much more. Do any of you have any experience in this area?"

Kelly laughed and said, "I know there is a heaven and a hell, and that we are all going one place or the other. I personally would like to go to heaven, and would like to explore the way to heaven."

Linda said, "I feel the same. I know less than anyone here. I know I must ask God to forgive my work at the saloon."

Leland put his hand over on Linda's and said, "We all need to ask for God's forgiveness for our sins."

Kelly said, "I don't know if God will forgive me, as I have killed many men. They were bad men, but the Bible says, 'Thou shall not kill." I think killing is the worse sin of all. You end someone's life before he has a chance to ask for forgiveness. You take him from his mother, father, brothers and sisters and sometimes wife and children. No, I don't think God can forgive me."

Leland said, "I was taught that there is no sin God will not forgive. If he forgave me, Kelly, I'm sure he will forgive you."

"Linda said, "That gives me hope. Why don't we get someone to teach us what we need to know?"

Cali said, "Let's go into town tomorrow and seek help."

Leland said, "I was waiting on you to get back to stand up for me, Kelly. Linda and I want to get married."

Kelly said, "We can do that when we are in town."

The next day they took Leland's buckboard into town. They went to the minister of the only church in town, but he had gone to Kansas City to attend his brother's funeral. One of the church members said, "There's an itinerate minister who is filling in for Brother Stewart. He may help you."

They found him and his name was Bobby Humphrey. He said, "Yes, I can marry you as I have gone through a seminary, and have been ordained. However, I wish to speak to you in private before there can be a ceremony."

Leland said, "I'm game. How about you Linda?"

"Let's do it."

The four of them went to the church. Pastor Humphrey said, "I just wanted to tell you some things about marriage before you plunge into it."

Leland said, "Maybe I should tell you about us. As you can tell, I'm a lot older than Linda. I have been a widower for over eleven years. I loved my wife dearly. We went to church back then. We all received Christ and were baptized."

Linda then broke in and said, "I don't want Leland to pretty my life up. I want you to know everything about me, as most people know what I was. I worked in a saloon as one of the girls men use. We met there, and found we liked each other. Leland needed a house cleaner and cook, and I wanted out of that life. I liked Leland a lot and suggested we live together. We did, and now he wants to make an honest woman out of me, because we found we love one another. So there you have it. I want to be forgiven for my sins and they are many. I'm not sure the Lord can forgive me, but I sure want Him to."

The pastor studied Linda awhile, then said, "God will forgive you, I can tell you that from experience. I won't go into my past, but I can assure you it was lurid. I wanted just what you want. I received Christ, and was born again. Every sin I ever committed was washed away by Jesus' blood. I can't tell you how thrilled I am to lead you to Christ. I wondered why God sent me on this trip, and now I know. It was for you, Linda."

Linda now had tears flowing down her cheeks, and Leland put his hand over to her hand. Pastor Humphrey said, "Do you repent of your sins and ask God to forgive you?"

Linda nodded and said, "I surely do."

Do you believe God sent his son, Jesus, to earth to die for your sins and mine?"

Linda nodded, as she couldn't answer. He then said, "Ask Jesus to come into your heart."

Linda said, "I just did."

Linda, you have been born again, and are the newest member of God's chosen people."

Leland said, "I have two other people, my son-in-law and his girlfriend. They want to know more about the Lord. Why don't you come with us to our ranch, and stay awhile. We need you to educate us further. Pastor Humphrey said, "I would love to. I'll pack some things, while you get a marriage license. We can then marry you in the church, and then go on to your place."

They were married an hour later. Only Kelly and Cali were there.

Kelly checked at the post office, and found he had a letter from Colonel Alfred. He opened it, and it was instructions for him to look into Barry Hanson in Houston. Being he wanted to go to Houston anyway, he wrote back that he would accept the mission.

They spent another three days with Pastor Humphrey, and at the end of that time, Kelly received Christ and was baptized in a horse trough.

Pastor Humphrey said, "It is fitting to be baptized in a horse trough, as Jesus was born in a manger.

Kelly felt much better about himself, now, as he knew God had forgiven his sins.

CHAPTER 18

FERRETING OUT A CULPRIT

He discussed the trip to Houston with Cali. She wanted to be there if Kelly found that any of her family was involved with her abduction. They decided to keep her out of sight.

Kelly felt that neither Hanson or Bridger knew him, so he could operate openly. He decided to talk to Hanson alone and use the ploy that they had arrested Captain Cruz. He would say that Cruz had confessed, and told them about Hanson to get a lighter sentence.

Kelly went to Hanson's office, and asked to speak to him about a private matter. He was invited into Hanson's office, and sat opposite of him with the door closed.

Kelly said, "I am a U. S. Marshal," and showed Hanson his badge. "We have arrested Captain Cruz for the kidnapping of Mrs. Cali Bridger. We have rescued her from a plantation in Cuba.

"Captain Cruz told us that you paid him to abduct her and take her out of the country. He made arrangements to sell her to Senor Esteban, a plantation owner in Cuba."

Hanson was in shock. He finally said, "I was told Cali had tuberculosis, and was in a sanitarium in Colorado."

"That was a cover story the attorney general's office sent you to cover her absents while we recovered Mrs. Bridger. Things will go easier for you if you confess. I can't promise you anything, but if you do confess, I will talk to the court about your cooperation, and ask for a lighter sentence.

"I would like you to write out a full confession in your own words, telling everyone who was involved, and their roles in this crime. As you are an assistant to Congressman Bridger, this will save him great embarrassment if you just make a confession and I take you back to Washington DC. If you don't, this is going to the front page of every news paper in Texas. I think you can understand what that will do to the career of the congressman."

"Hanson said, "I need a lawyer. I will not do anything until I see a lawyer."

"Oh yes, you will do something, I will arrest you and call a press conference and display you, so photos can be taken."

"That's blackmail!" Hanson shouted.

"Call it what you may, but either write out the confession, or I'll take you out of here in handcuffs. If you write out a confession, we will just leave, and you can tell your secretary that you are going to Washington DC on business. Once there, we will handle this as quietly as we can, if Congressman Bridger is not involved."

"I can promise you he wasn't. He would probably kill me, if he knew what I did. I will write the confession and go with you. When I get there I will send back my resignation to Congressman Bridger."

Hanson wrote the confession, He had already decided not to involve Robert Bridger, as he would be his only source of influence and help once in jail. He would write him a letter explaining what had happened, and that he was taking the rap for them.

Hanson said, "Can we go by my house. I need to pack and tell my wife I am going on an extended trip. I will tell her I will write her about it when I get there."

They left and went to Hanson's home. He introduced Kelly as a business associate. He told his wife he didn't know how long he would be gone, but that he would write as soon as he knew that.

They went by the hotel and Kelly had a bell boy take a message to Cali. It said, "Hide in the bathroom. I am bringing Hanson to our room and don't want him to see you. Go back to your home and tell them you were let out of the sanitarium, and had no trace of tuberculosis anymore."

Kelly threw his things in his suitcase, and they were off. They caught a ship to New York and a train to Washington DC. Kelly handed over Hanson and his confession to Colonel Alfred. Kelly explained that Hanson had been cooperative, and that ought to weigh in his favor when a sentence was handed down.

Kelly said, "Mr. Hanson wants this to be handled as quietly as possible, because he has sworn that Congressman Bridger was not involved. You can read that in the confession. Hanson has stated that he wants to appear only before a judge, and be sentenced as quietly as possible as not to affect Congressman Bridger's career."

It was handled quietly and Hanson was sentenced to fifteen years at hard labor, however, after Kelly testified on Bridger's behalf, the sentence was reduced to ten years.

Hanson never knew that Cruz was still at large. The time for the trial and all the procedures took only a month, as it was expedited through the system. The newspapers had written that a man, named Barry Hanson, was convicted of conspiracy to a kidnapping, and was sentenced to ten years. The Bridger name was never mentioned in the press as they never connected Hansen with Congressman Bridger.

Cali went home and explained that she was now cured. She showed no signs of tuberculosis, and that it must have been just a bad cold, misdiagnosed. Things in Houston just went on as usual. Hanson's letter to Congressman Bridger stated that he had been given an offer in England that he couldn't refuse. Congressman Bridger didn't miss him that much, and Hanson's wife got a letter telling her about the same thing, but that he would send for her in a few months. He then wrote Robert Bridger telling him the whole story, and that he had kept him and Max out of it.

Meanwhile, Captain Cruz had gone to a port in Trinidad where a ship repair yard was located. He had his ship repainted and new features put aboard, that changed the profile of the *Simon Bolivar*. He went to the harbormaster, and for two hundred dollars, had the name of his ship changed to the *Nymph*. He then had his own name changed to Carlos Cantos. He thought he was now in the clear.

Kelly was now back in New York trading stocks. However, he still spent most of his spare time at the docks interviewing sailors. He knew that sooner or later someone would have news of Captain Cruz and his ship.

Cali wrote that she was divorcing Bridger. Their divorce was handled very quietly as Max knew a judge, who granted them an annulment. Cali just quietly moved to New York where she and Kelly were married. They decided against a honeymoon and didn't inform Cali's family about her change in spouses. Kelly introduced Coy to Cali. Coy was delighted that she was as enthusiastic as Kelly about trading stocks. The three had lunch every day and spent the afternoon looking into stocks. They both found that Cali was astute in trading and asked her advice quite often.

Kelly spent a lot of time at the wharf and the saloons there. He finally received a tip that the *Simon Bolivar's* new name was the *Nymph*, out of Trinidad. That day Kelly sent a telegram to Colonel Alfred telling him about the ship changing names and that she was based in Trinidad.

Colonel Alfred discussed it with the attorney general and his staff. It was then settled that Kelly be sent to Trinidad and try to get the Nymph's sailing schedule. If it ever included an American port, the ship would be taken by the navy and Captain Cruz arrested.

Kelly came home and said, "How would you like to go to Trinidad?" "Where is that?" Cali asked.

It's an Island in the Caribbean ocean. It has a great climate, and being we are freezing here in New York, it will be a great change." They packed and left as soon as they could catch a ship that would stop there.

Trinidad was a friendly place, but nearly everyone was a native. They did find a hotel that was nice. The food was pretty good, although much different. Cali stayed at the hotel while Kelly went to the harbormaster to get a line on the Nymph.

The harbormaster showed that the ship was due to be back in ten days. It would stay in Trinidad a week, then go to Havana, Tampa Bay and lastly Houston, before returning.

They waited three days before they could book passage to Miami. There Kelly wired Colonel Alfred that the Nymph would be in Houston in two weeks and that he was headed there now.

Alfred wired back that a Major Brock and a company of men, with orders to accommodate U. S. Marshal Kelly Andrews in boarding a ship to arrest Captain Cruz.

Kelly and Cali arrived in Houston and found that a U. S. Navy ship was there. Kelly talked to her captain. He was due to return to Virginia in two weeks. After several wires, the captain of the man-of-war was ordered to escort the Nymph to the navy yard at Norfolk and be confiscated.

Kelly had the company of soldiers waiting at the dock. The U. S. naval ship came behind the Nymph as she docked, blocking any attempt to escape. Kelly led the company of men aboard and Captain Cruz, aka Captain Cantos, was arrested without incident. He was put in the brig of the man-of-war along with several of his men. They were taken to Washington DC, where they were prosecuted. Cruz was given twenty years at hard labor, and put in the same federal prison as Hanson.

When they returned, Kelly spoke to Colonel Alfred and they decided not to pursue anyone else in the crime.

Kelly was granted a leave of absence and they decided to return to New York City and lead a simple life.

***

Estabon knew he was in trouble, and that he might very well be arrested by the king of Spain. He transferred ownership of his plantation to his sister, who was now a widow. She adored Estabon and told him not to worry, that she would hold his property until the heat was off him.

He had another place on an island close to Cuba. It was not claimed by any country, and that's why he built there. His house wasn't as elaborate as his Cuban mansion, but he had most of the amenities that he was used to. He brought his girls and servants with him. Before he left he brought several pounds of gold and silver with him, so he could do business.

He was on the island now, and his girls seemed to like it, as it was close to the beach and they loved to swim in the serf. He always made them go nude. He would sit in a chair under a cluster of palm trees and watch them, while he sipped a fruit drink. He began thinking of how he might get back at the man who took Cali from him.

Estabon hired a detective to trace down Kelly. It was not a hard job, and his man traced him to New York City. He found that he was now married to Cali, and that he spent a lot of his time at the New York Stock Exchange. He wasn't interested in Cali, and he generally only kept a girl for a year or so anyway. But, he was interested in getting Kelly Andrews and paying him back for the trouble he had caused him.

He thought he could kidnap Kelly, but he wanted to exact a punishment that fit the crime. He didn't want to kill Kelly, as that would be too easy on him. He wanted him to suffer living in terrible conditions. He thought of sending him to the silver mines in Mexico, where a man could live about five years before they worked him to death. However, that was not good enough. He then thought of the mines in China, where he had sent dissident servants or people, who owed him money, and could not pay. He thought, *"I need an unusual punishment where I can witness it once in awhile. This will take me some time to figure just the right punishment. I want him to live in fear while being starved. I want him too cold and too hot. I would like him to be deprived of sleep."*

He then thought of building a prison for Kelly. It would have walls he could never climb. He could put snakes that had the venom removed, so Kelly would think he was always in danger. He would take all his clothes from him, and keep him in the sun. He would furnish him water that tasted so bad he could barely swallow it. His food would have worms through it.

Estabon did understand that some people really loved one another, and he thought Kelly really loved Cali. He would build a room adjoining Kelly's prison. The wall between the two rooms would be two feet thick with insulation, so that the Cali's room was soundproof. A window would be put between the common wall. It would be high enough in Cali's room so she could not see through it. He would build a platform in Kelly's prison so he could climb up and view into Cali's room. Kelly would then be able to see what went on in Cali's room, but she would be unaware that Kelly could see into her room. The thickness of the glass was four inches so no sound could come from there either. Estabon had another window cut into another room, so he could observe her.

The unsheltered prison that Kelly occupied had a chair on the platform, so Kelly could sit while he observed Cali. That was all the furniture that was in Kelly's walled prison. It was open to the sun and had a floor of cliché that was very hard. As Kelly had no tools, it would be impossible to dig his way out.

Estabon would then capture them both and bring them to his island. He smiled to himself, as he thought of the things he would have his men do to Cali. This punishment would probably be more economical, also.

Estabon put his plan into motion. He found that Cruz had been arrested, so he went to another captain named Lloyd Butcher. He was the captain who had brought him Chin. He told him he would give him a thousand American dollars to kidnap two people from New York, and bring them to him. Butcher hired a gang to bring the two people to him aboard his ship, *The Haitian*. This gang was an Irish gang and they came into Kelly's apartment and used ether on them. They awoke at sea. They were in separate rooms, so then didn't know the other was aboard. However, they both reasoned that this was probably the case. They also reasoned that it was Estabon, who paid for the abduction.

Kelly only had a pair of pants and a short sleeved shirt.

Six days later they were put into Estabon's prison. They had not seen Estabon nor each others, and didn't really know if it were Estabon who had abducted them.

Estabon had been raised by his father. His father was a cruel man and Estabon witnessed a lot of his cruelty. His father liked his son, Jaime, but never doted on him, as he was more interested in his own pleasure. They were wealthy, and could have about anything they wanted.

When Estabon was twenty, his father bought him the plantation in Cuba, and saw that Estabon and his sister were out of his hair. Estabon's sister, Myra, loved Estabon as he took care of her, and she was the only relative he had in Cuba. Estabon and Myra were cramping their father's style, now, and he wanted rid of them. Thus the plantation. He saw that they had all the money they could ever spend, as his family had brought many ships from South America filled with gold.

Myra married and lived in Havana. Her husband worked for Estabon, but was caught stealing from him. Estabon had him killed, and made it look like an accident. Myra was not all that heart broken, as she had found that her husband was keeping a younger woman as his mistress. This killed the love she had for him.

When Cali and Kelly arrived on the island, they thought that maybe it was not Estabon who took them. Cali's room was nicely furnished. A maid came three times a day to feed her and empty her chamber pots. She was always accompanied by a huge man.

Kelly's prison had twelve foot walls and bare ground that was so hard it was like concrete. There were some bushes but no way to get out of the sun, except the shade the walls provided.

Immediately, Kelly could see Cali. He banged on the glass, but could tell she could not hear him. He did enjoy watching her as he had nothing else to do.

That night after everyone was asleep, Kelly began to work out. He would run in place for a half hour each night. He would do pushups, and sit ups for another half hour. He was getting into shape.

At the night meal, he would sit on his chair and watch Cali. The first night after Cali had eaten, a Chinese man came into the room. He had two pipes. One for himself and one for Cali. He would talk to Cali and encourage her to smoke with him. Nearly at once, Kelly knew that the pipe contained opium.

He knew that Cali probably had never heard of the drug. The only way Kelly knew about it, was from a man he was in the service with. The man had lived in China and told how many of the Chinese were addicted to smoking opium.

There was no way to tell Cali, and he watched day after day as she smoked with the Chinese man. He knew he must get her out of there before she became addicted.

Cali began to look forward to smoking the opium. She began to want it over anything, even eating. She couldn't wait for the Chinese man to come each night.

Kelly could tell that she was changing. He knew he must do something, even if it cost him his life.

It was now into the fourth week. Instead of the Chinese man coming after supper, two of the guards appeared. They had the pipe that Cali now craved. Kelly could see the men talking to her, and she began to disrobe. He watched as one of the guards had her. They then gave her several puffs of the opium pipe. She then did the other guard, and they left the pipe with her.

Kelly knew that Estabon was behind this. He was torturing them both. Kelly made up his mind that he had to do something. He had been trained to fight, but the guard who came with the maid, was a huge man, and seemed fairly agile.

The next night, two other guards came and they talked to her and she disrobed and laid over her table face down. One of the guards took her from behind, then gave her a few puffs of the pipe. Then the other guard took her and then left her the pipe.

This was enough for Kelly. He swore he would take on the huge guard that was with the woman who brought him his food.

Cali seemed to be in a stupor most of the day. He knew the man who always came with the maid, and he was six to ten inches taller than Kelly, and outweighed him by over a fifty pounds. Kelly knew he must do something to stop what Cali was going through.

When the maid came that night, Kelly walked to her as he always had, but then swiftly kicked the guard in the groin. The man cried out with pain. Kelly then kicked in his knee so hard that his knee cap was knocked out of place. As the man bent over, Kelly kicked him in the head, and he was out cold. The maid just stood there in stark terror. He turned to the maid and said, "If you help me, I will not kill you, but if I even suspicion you are not helping me, I'll kill you."

She understood and Kelly asked, "Where are the guards?"

"There is one guarding the front door and one guarding the backdoor. Both are armed with a rifle."

"Are there any guards in the house?" She shook her head.

"Where is Estabon at this time?"

"He is eating dinner with his girls."

"Does he have a pistol in his room."

She said, "I don't know."

"Raise you voice, and ask the guard at the back to come help you. I'll be just around the corner. If he has any suspicion that something is wrong, I'll kill you. Do you understand?"

The maid was terrified, as she thought the bodyguard on the floor was dead. She called, "Eduardo, would you come help me?"

"In just a second or two, Eduardo came, and as he came near, Kelly stepped out and rendered him unconscious in a spit second. They then locked the two guards in Kelly's prison.

Kelly said, "We will go to the front, and you call that guard, also, to come help you. Don't go past the corner of the house. I will be right behind you." She called the guard, and as he rounded the corner, Kelly hit him with the butt of the other guards rifle so hard it split his skull open.

Kelly then said, "Help me drag him into my prison. When they had all three in his prison he locked the door and said, "Take me to the dining room."

She led the way. As they came to the dining room two women servants backed up knowing there was real trouble. Kelly came into the room, but Estabon had his back to the door. Kelly said, "Everyone at the table lie on the floor, or I will shoot you."

Estabon knew it was Kelly. He and the girls laid on the floor along with the two women servants. Kelly propped his rifle against the wall and frisked Estabon. He had no weapon.

Kelly then said, "I want everyone to come with me to where you are keeping Cali. I will lock you in her room." They all went quietly, as Estabon knew the danger of not following Kelly's orders to the letter.

The door was opened and Cali came to the door. She was nearly in a stupor and thought Estabon was bring her a pipe. She then saw the girls and servants with Kelly behind them.

He said, "Come out quickly, Cali."

She did what he said, then Kelly said to the maid, "You stay with us." He then locked the door on the rest. Estabon had built the room so no one could escape it.

Kelly said to the maid, "How many more guards are on the grounds?"

"Two more. They are at the gate."

"Go tell them that Senor Estabon wants them at the house. I will shoot you in the back if I think you're trying to tip them off."

The maid was way past not cooperating with what she was asked to do. She called the two guards, and they came to the house only to see a rifle pointed at them. Kelly said, "Follow the maid. I want them in the place I was in. The maid turned and went out the front door with the two guards following her. When the maid opened the door, the guards saw the one guard lying dead with his head split open and an other guard that was crippled. This told them that Kelly would kill them instantly if they tried anything. The entered the prison, and Kelly locked them in. He and the maid went back into the house.

Kelly said, "I haven't eaten yet, so let's sit down and eat."

Kelly sat at the end of the table so he could watch the door. He said, "That means you, too," to the maid, who quickly sat down.

Cali said, "Please bring me a pipe. I need it badly."

Kelly turned to the maid and said, What do they call you?"

"Lora."

"Are there other guards on the Island?"

"Yes. There are four more that live in a building near the beach."

"When will those guards come on duty?"

"At eight o'clock."

Cali again said, "Kelly I need my pipe. Please get it for me. You can't know how I need it." Kelly just ignored her.

Kelly looked at the clock on the wall and it was just after seven. He wanted to go through Estabon's house and get any weapons he might have. They finished eating and then began the search. Cali had not touched a thing on her plate. She just stared at the wall.

Kelly found a pistol in Estabon's room and that was all. The pistol was in a scabbard that had many bullets in the belt. He had the maid stack all the rifles in the dining room. He took each and with the corner of the door and the wall, bent the barrels so they were rendered useless. He kept two rifles and had his pistol.

Kelly went outside to see where he wanted to accost the guards when they arrived. He asked the maid if the guards were ever early, and she said she didn't know.

Kelly looked over at Cali and said, "Are you okay?"

"No, all I want is my pipe. I need it badly."

"I'm sorry, but there will be no more pipes. It's opium, and you are addicted to it. I think in a few days you won't need it anymore."

"I need it now. Please let me have it. I will stop tomorrow."

"No, you have stopped today. Try drinking some whiskey. That will help dull your desire for opium."

Kelly looked at the maid and said, "Fix her a drink, and you can have one, too."

The maid smiled for the first time, and went to a liquor cabinet and then turned and said, "Do you want one, too?"

"No, just you and Cali have one."

The maid fixed Cali whiskey and water, but the maid drank rum and cola. Kelly said, "Are you on our side, now?"

The maid said, "I am. Estabon is an evil man. I heard what he had his men do to your wife. With the opium, she would probably do anything for a pipe of opium."

Cali didn't say a word, she just stared ahead and drank. She asked for another drink, as she was now hurting. Kelly said, "Take care of her, I must meet the guards."

Kelly stood outside the gate with his cap of a guard pulled down, so that it hid his face. He had the pistol hidden behind his leg. He could see four guards coming. They were talking among themselves, and didn't pay Kelly much attention until they were within twenty feet of Kelly. Kelly then pulled out the gun, and shot over their heads. He said, "Do exactly as I say or I'll kill you." All the guards dropped their rifles and put their hands up.

Kelly marched them back to the house and told the maid to come with him with the keys. He had the maid open the door with Kelly holding a pistol at the door. The guards were put with the other guards, and the maid locked the door again.

Kelly said, "Let's go get that Asian girl. The maid opened the door, and Kelly said, "Chin, come out." She did, and then the maid closed and locked the door again.

Kelly said, "You want to help us, or are you loyal to Estabon?"

"I hate him. I wish you would kill him. If you don't want to do it, let me have your pistol and I will."

"No, I want him to go to Cuba, as there is a warrant from the King of Spain. He will put Estabon in a Spanish prison. The other inmates will like to have a good looking man like Estabon."

Chin began to get it the picture and said, "Yes, that is what I would like. He can then be used like a woman like he used us."

Kelly said, "Do the two other girls want away from Estabon?"

"No, they love him."

"Well, we'll leave them for the guards, and we'll take Estabon with us."

He looked at the maid and said, "Is there anyone else on this island?"

"No, it's a small island. There is a boat that comes every Monday. It generally comes after lunch. It comes from the mainland with food and supplies. Senor Estabon has a sailboat, but no one knows how to man it, and it is very small."

Chin said, "This is Sunday, so the boat will be here tomorrow, probably just after lunch."

"We will need to feed them before we leave. Lora, you must stay and feed them. Don't unlock them until we are at sea."

They met the boat with Estabon tied up. Kelly showed the captain his badge and said a warrant for Estabon's arrest had been issued, by the king of Spain.

Kelly turned to the maid who had helped them and handed her the keys. He said, "After we have sailed, unlock the doors."

"The maid said, "I don't think anyone liked Senor Estabon, we all just tolerated him because he paid us well."

They arrived in Havana and turned Estabon over to the authorities.

CHAPTER 19

A NEW ASSIGNMENT

As they were sailing back, Cali was very quiet. She drank a lot during the day as she still wanted her pipe. Knowing she couldn't have it, she drank to quell her desire. She was drunk most of the time. She ate very little, but Kelly encouraged her as he said, "The only way to curb your desire for opium is to eat, and try to get back to where you were."

Kelly never told her what he had seen. She was barely aware of it, herself. She just remembered how much she desired her pipe.

Kelly asked, "Do you want to go back to Houston?"

"No, we might run into Max. I don't want to ever see him again.

Try to think of a place you would like to go or maybe live."

"At this point, I don't care where I live. All I can think of is how much I want my pipe."

Kelly said, "I used to think of living on some island in the Caribbean, but Estabon ruined that for me. I don't want to even think of him or that place again. I'll take that back, I do get pleasure thinking of what will happen to him in that Spanish prison. By the way, what are we going to do with Chin?"

Cali didn't even answer, she just stared at the wall and took another drink.

"I'll ask her where she wants to go, and give her enough money to live on for few months. I need to check in with Colonel Alfred. I hope they won't have another assignment for me. I will tell him I need a rest."

They docked in New York City and took a train to Washington DC. At Langley, Colonel Alfred was pleased to see them both. He told Kelly that nothing was going on that needed his expertise. Cali asked about Max and his father.

Alfred said, "Max isn't so popular anymore as many of his escapades have reached the press with one woman suing him. I doubt if he will be reelected if he even runs."

After they were on their way, Kelly said, "Let's go back to New York City for a few weeks then figure out where we would like to visit."

Cali didn't even answer. They returned and Kelly stayed right with her and slowly she began to talk again. Not much, but she now wasn't just thinking of her pipe. She still drank quite a bit and slept a lot.

Starting the third week in New York, Kelly said, "How would you like to visit the deep South. I've always wanted to go to Savanna, Georgia. I've heard that it's an interesting place."

"She just nodded then said, "I know I need to stop drinking so much. I still long for my pipe, but I know I can't do that anymore. Maybe my drinking will let up in a new place."

They decided to take a ship as the accommodations were excellent. There was gambling going on and after their dinner they stood watching. The stakes were not outstanding, but the table sat seven men.

They were far enough away to see the game, but could whisper comments without being heard. One man seemed to play most of his hands. He was well dressed, but not over dressed. He said nothing' and his expression never changed. The other players were not card sharks, just ordinary players. Some were not so swift in their play.

Kelly watched the man with most of the chips carefully, especially when he dealt. He was adroit with his skill in dealing. Not flashy, but efficient and fast. Kelly looked to see if he had a partner, but could not see the slightest move that would indicate one. He seemed to be legit in his playing, just astute in playing the cards dealt him.

Cali had drank three drinks and said, "I'm tired and need to go to bed. You stay as you enjoy watching. After watching another ten minutes, he thought he would just see that Cali was okay. He left and when he returned to their room, Cali was already asleep. He then returned to the game. After a man dropped out, Kelly took his place. He folded his first two hands. The deal was now to him, but as usual he passed the deal.

Kelly was dealt three nines on the next deal. Bets were made before they received cards. When it came to Kelly, he upped the bet and three players dropped out. One of the players just to his left upped the raise. The card player stayed in, but had never raised.

Kelly asked for one card. The dealer, who had raised him asked for one also. The card player took one. It was at this point that the card player put out his little finger only a small space, then raised the pot twenty dollars.

Kelly picked up his one card and it was another nine. He just called the card player, but the man to his left, who had started the raising, called and raised another twenty. The card player called and raised again.

Kelly folded, and was met by a slight surprise from the card player, and a slack jaw from the player to his left. He just called. The card player had only a pair of jacks. The dealer had to show his hand and it was four tens.

Kelly decided the game was rigged, so he retired to his room.

Cali was deep in sleep. Kelly poured himself a drink and began to think of what had happened to them. They had not had sex since they had been abducted. Cali was not interested in anything. She ate very little.

Kelly knew she was going through a deep depression. She probably didn't even remember the guards using her. She was stupefied by then, with her craving for opium. She still was to a certain extent, but alcohol had dulled some of her cravings. He knew she didn't need or want sex. He understood that. Her emotions had been blunted, and it would take time for her to get back where she was. Maybe she would never get back. He would just have to wait and see.

Savanna was better than he had imagined. The Azaleas were in bloom, and the many mansions were beautiful. There were also many shops with beautiful dresses. He gave Cali a couple of hundred dollars and told her to shop until she was exhausted. He said, "I'll be in that coffee shop I showed you. I need to write a card to the Colonel and then read the financial page and see how much I'm losing there."

She only nodded, then turned and left.

Kelly sat at a table and read the financial page and drank a cup of coffee. He was there only a few minutes when a voice from behind him said, "Don't turn around, but I need you to help me." It was a woman's voice that resonated smoothly. She had a slight southern drawl.

She said, "I know who you are, as I was in Joplin a few years ago when you foiled those three bank robbers. Just by coincidence I was in Julesburg when the *Wild Bunch* appeared. My husband, just like your wife, was killed by them. Since then, you and I have remarried. I saw you briefly just before the shooting started. When the bandits were killed, I knew you were back of it, somehow. I could not see how, but I knew."

"So how can I help you, Miss... ...."

"Mrs. Lang. My husband is trying to kill me. I don't have any proof, but three times I have nearly been killed in the past two months. I inherited a substantial legacy from my first husband. He was a cattle buyer. I had no idea he was that wealthy. His father was a Wall Street broker who left Lenny a fortune.

"I married Darwin on the rebound. He is handsome and says all the right things and has impeccable manners. I was charmed, so I didn't see the dark side of him. With a little investigation from a Pinkerton man, I found he had done away with two other wives.

"I'm scared and had no place to turn, until just by chance I saw you come out of your hotel room with your wife. I then saw a light at the end of the tunnel. Will you help protect me while I seek a divorce? I will pay you ten thousand dollars."

"That is a lot of money. I was about to turn you down, but that amount of money has made me your bodyguard."

About that time Cali came into the coffee house. She had just one package. She said, "I just realized, I don't have any room for anything. However, I couldn't pass up this gown," and she indicated the package she had.

Kelly said, "I hate to disappoint you, but I have another assignment. I must send you back to New York City for awhile. I don't think this assignment will be that long, but it could last up to a month. You might be in harms way if you stayed. I can't tell you where I'm going, but I will contact you by letter in a week or so. Is that alright?"

"Well, a man has to work to live in the style we are accustom. I will visit my parents. That way you won't have to visit them with me."

"Can you leave today?"

"Yes, I know the ship will leave at around noon. You can see me off?"

As the ship pulled away, and he could no longer see Cali, Mrs. Lang stepped to Kelly's side."

She said, "My given name is Lynda, may I call you, Kelly?"

"I would like that."

Lynda was a beauty. Kelly wondered how he hadn't noticed her in Joplin or Julesburg. Anyone would have noticed her and taken a second look. She took Kelly's arm as they left the dock.

They hadn't walked two blocks until they met Darwin Lang. He said with a smile on his face, "Already stepping out on me, are you, Lynda?"

"Darwin, this is my cousin Kelly Andrews. I had no idea he was here in Savanna. We just put his wife on the ship back to New York."

Kelly put out his hand and Darwin took it as they both smiled. Darwin said, "What do you do, Mr. Kelly?"

"I dabble in the market, and take assignment for cash."

"What are you into now?"

"An assignment, but I can't elaborate."

"Must be interesting work."

"Yes, and sometimes deadly."

This brought a shocked look to Darwin's face as he thought of the two near misses he had caused to take Lynda's life. He realized that this man was dangerous. He might be working on another case, but these kind of men were astute, and could smell out danger as it was their business.

Darwin said, "Well, good luck. Lynda and I are leaving tomorrow."

Lynda said, "No, I've decided to stay with Kelly for a week or so, to catch up on old times."

"Well, I'm telling you, we are leaving!"

"I hope you have a good time, I'm leaving you Darwin. I'm seeking a divorce. So run along."

Darwin turned and left in a huff. He thought, *I'll teach that bitch a lesson before I leave.* Then he thought, *"Maybe I should just leave. That Andrews may be deadly."*

Lynda said, "I hope you will stay with me tonight. I'm sure he will pull something. He won't leave me without getting something."

"Yes, even if you offered him money, he would want more. Have you thought about having a will that would leave him nothing if you die, then give him a copy?"

"No, that's why I have you. You think of the things I should do. You have already earned your money. Let's go to a lawyer now."

They went to the courthouse and asked a clerk who the smartest lawyer was in Savanna."

He whispered, "I'm not suppose to tell people these things, but if it were me, I would go to Harold Moseley. He's located just across the street.

They thanked him, and went across the street and found Moseley's office. He had a clerk. After being consulted, they were shown into an elaborate office. Moseley stood and said, "How may I help you?"

Lynda said, "I want to divorce my husband, but before anything, I want a will that leaves him nothing if I die."

Kelly smiled and said, "I'm not her husband," and they all laughed.

"I would say a quite tolerant one if you were."

After giving Moseley all the facts he said, "I'll have the will ready tomorrow and process the paper work for your divorce tomorrow, also. He then gave Lynda the bill and she paid him with a check. They then left.

Kelly said, "I suggest we stay at a conservative hotel that has some security. I will order a room with two beds."

They hired a hack and he drove them to a hotel that the hack recommended. It was out of the way some, but in a nice neighborhood. They checked in as Mr. and Mrs. Sanders. They then went out and bought the things they would need to spend the night. After delivering these to the hotel they went to the restaurant in the hotel. The food was plain, but healthy. Kelly put her in their new hotel room, then left and checked out of his old hotel with his luggage and guns. When he returned, Lynda was in a robe and looked lovely."

Kelly put a chair under the knob of the door. In his luggage he had a quart of brandy and poured them both two fingers in the glasses provided by the hotel.

Lynda said, "Are you plying me with liquor?"

"Yes, you will sleep better. I don't think your husband knows where we are, but you never know."

Kelly pushed the beds away from the window, should someone try to shoot through it. They were also not against the wall.

Lynda said, "You are a very careful man, Kelly. I wish you were single."

"I would think you were tired of men."

"No, I need a man, like most men need a woman. I have always been hot blooded. I wish I weren't, but it's just a fact. Darwin was a good lover and I thought I had a good man, but he's overcome with greed. He wasn't satisfied with sharing my wealth, he wanted it all."

The hotel only had one bathroom that served the floor, so Kelly stood guard while Lynda bathed and used the facility. Kelly took her back to the room and he returned and bathed. When he returned to their room, Lynda said, "Can a goodnight kiss be included with your service?"

"Ten thousand dollars will provide that service, but it stops there. I still honor my wife."

"They were standing and Kelly took her in his arms. She kissed him a passionate kiss. After they pulled away, Kelly said, "You kiss a lot like my first wife, Patty. We met in a most unusual way."

"Please tell me about it."

"No, that is just for us."

After breakfast, they went back to Moseley's for the will. He had four copies for them. He said, "One will be filed with the County Clerk. One is for my files, one is for you, and you can deliver the other to your husband."

Kelly said, "Let's go to his hotel and deliver his copy of the will. You can stay at the end of the hall, and if he comes to the door, I will give him his copy. You can just stay at the corner, out of sight, and witness me giving it to him."

It went like Kelly had predicted. Darwin answered the door, and Kelly handed him a copy of the will. Darwin read it there, as it was short and to the point. It was easy to see he would not receive a cent if Lynda died.

Darwin said, "Well, this may preclude me from any of her fortune by the will, but we will see what a divorce brings."

Kelly said, "I guess you will have to come up with something better than accidents, now."

Darwin said, "We will see who has the last laugh."

Kelly said, "You know Darwin, you had better start looking out for accidents yourself. This can work both ways, you know. Lynda may not get any money from your death, but she would get some satisfaction, and not have to go through a divorce."

Darwin was shocked. He had never thought of an accident happening to him. He also knew Kelly was a dangerous man. He shut the door in a hurry."

Lynda laughed as they left the hotel. Kelly said, "You are safe for awhile, now. Let's go ask Moseley if Darwin could get any of your money in the divorce."

Moseley said, "You had the wealth before you married Darwin. I can't see how any judge could award him anything. However, you could safeguard that by giving all of your wealth to a trusted relative until the divorce is settled."

"I know of only one person I would trust, and that is Mr. Andrews here."

"Lynda, I don't want that responsibility. How do you know I won't leave you with nothing?"

"I know. After meeting you, I know your integrity." They were now at Moseley's office.

When they left, Lynda said, "That Moseley is a smart man. He made a document giving you all my assets until one day after the divorce was final, then I would obtain my assets again by the document you signed."

As they were walking back to their hotel, They saw a boy about fifteen, walking toward them. Kelly stopped him and said, "How would you like to make two dollars?"

The boy smiled and said, "Who do I have to kill?"

They all three laughed and Kelly said, "I want you to be a detective. There is a man who may take the ship that will leave the docks at noon tomorrow. I will give you a dollar to give to the hotel clerk. Go to the clerk and tell him you will give him a dollar if he will point out Mr. Darwin Lang to you. See if the man checks out of the hotel around ten tomorrow. You must be there at eight a. m. to make sure you don't miss him. I will give you a dollar now, and a dollar when you follow him to his ship. If he doesn't check out, you will earn the dollar anyway. Come to my hotel at one o'clock and let me know how it comes out. I will be in the lobby at the Savanna Hotel. Can you handle it?"

"I'm your boy."

Kelly handed him two dollars and the boy took off.

"I don't think Darwin can get my money. I will pay you off, and let you go your way. I will always cherish meeting you."

At one o'clock the boy was at the lobby and said, "He got on the ship. I waited until it started out of the bay, before I left."

Kelly handed him a dollar and the boy thanked him and took off.

CHAPTER 20

THE CONFESSION

Kelly left the day after Darwin left. He wondered if he should tell Cali about Lynda. He remembered Lynda's telling him to not tell her. He thought it prudent. He had been never lied to her, but he didn't see not telling her about his assignment was lying.

Kelly came to New York City expecting Cali to be in Boston. He was just entering their apartment when he saw Cali. She gave him a brief hug then poured herself a drink. She slugged that down then poured another. She said, "You had better have one yourself, as I have something to tell you."

Kelly knew this couldn't be good, so he poured himself a stiff drink or rye.

They were now seated in two soft chairs opposite of one another. Cali didn't say anything for awhile, as she just drank her second drink. She then said, "Pour us another drink, Kelly, we are both going to need a few. I have something I must tell you."

Kelly poured the drinks and she started.

"On my way back to Boston, I was seated at the captain's table next to a handsome man. When dinner was over he asked me to the lounge where we had several drinks. We were talking about jewelry as he dealt in them. He said he had a beautiful diamond necklace he wanted to show me.

"We went to his room, and he showed me an array of beautiful bracelets, rings and necklaces. We had a couple drinks there, and we were both feeling it. He wanted to put a beautiful necklace on me, so I stood. He put the necklace on me. I turned around and he kissed me. The kiss went on and on. I thought of you, but wanted this man. I wanted to hurt you. I don't know why, but I did. I pulled the guy to bed, and we made love. We then fell asleep. The next morning I was stone sober, and made love to him again, because I wanted it.

"We docked at noon and I can't even remember his name. I think he was married also. I hate what I did, but there it is. If you want to leave me, I wouldn't blame you. What's bad is I questioned myself, and tried to relive those moments. It was like I wanted to do it, because of you. I also wanted the pleasure of a strange man. I wanted that pleasure, and couldn't stop myself even knowing the consequence. I have never had that feeling before. I now wonder if I can be true to you in the future."

"That is an incredible story. I can see why you wanted to hurt me. I dumped you off while you were going through a traumatic time. I deserved it. I don't even blame you for having sex with him. You probably needed the sex. It may help in the healing process. I don't condemn you. It happened. You couldn't do anything about it, so who is hurt. I still love you like I always did. I would never leave you. I love you. Try to forget about it. When you do think about it, put my face on the man, and feel good about it."

"Do you think my addition to opium might have changed me. Estabon did terrible things to me during my addition and I enjoyed them. I even looked forward to them."

"Yes, it was the opium. You had such a desire for it that it made anything that was connected to it desirable. That may have changed you some, but I think over time we will get back to where we were."

"I don't know. I know I've changed. Opium is a terrible thing. I still want it, even though I know what it does to you. I don't desire it as much, and the desire is much less now, but it may always rule me in other areas. I found out how weak I was. That is what hurt the most is how loose I've become. From what I know about myself now, I think I will cheat on you again."

"Cali, you have been through a trying time. I think you hate Estabon and somehow you are putting me with him as you want to strike back. I don't think the sex is what caused you to do what you did. It is getting back at all the things that happened to you. Time is really a good cure. I think you will get back to where you were. I will be here for you."

"I know you are a good man, but I don't want you now. I hope I will in the future, but right now I don't want you around. I think you are right about me confusing you with Estabon and maybe even Max."

"Please don't ever compare me to Max. He's the lowest form of life. I've even thought about killing him."

"This really shocked Cali. She said, "Please never think like that. He's not worth killing."

They slept together that night, but didn't even kiss. Kelly now knew the depth of Cali's despair. He thought, *"I must go away and let her sort this out for herself. She may have sex with a dozen men, who knows. Maybe with me gone she won't hate me as much. Right now she hates me. I can see it in her eyes."*

The next morning Cali said, "I think we should be apart for awhile. I don't know how long, but I think we need to be apart."

"Have you lost the magic you once said we had?"

"I think I have. I need to reassess myself. To do that I need to be away from you for awhile. It's not your fault. This is all on me. But I need the space. Do you understand?"

"Not really. We once were close, but just like that, we're not. It was like when you first saw me. You were instantly in love. Now, you don't know if you're in love with me or not. You have changed. Just like that. True love is not like that. True love is lasting. I don't know if you have ever loved me or if it was just a phase. Take your time. I'm leaving for the west. I don't know if I will contact you again, we'll just have to see." While he was talking he had been packing. He walked out without saying another word.

Cali sat alone for awhile and began to cry. This was not what she wanted. She now felt the remorse. She had told him she needed to be away from him, but now she didn't. She thought she had lost the love of her life. It was like when she found out that Cooper had been killed. She couldn't do anything that would have stopped that, but this time she had caused the loss. She just hadn't thought it through.

She thought, *"I will wait for one year, before I do anything. If at the end of that time he has not come back, I will kill myself. I have surely made a mess of this life. I had the best man in the world and drove him away. What a fool I am. There went my happiness. I just threw him away.*

***

Kelly was so distraught he hardly knew what he was doing. He thought, *"This is my punishment for not seeing how she needed me. What was I thinking. I think she's right. I need some time to reassess myself, too. Who am I. I was able to resist Lynda, but I wanted her dearly. Maybe the next time I will succumb to a woman's wiles. I used to be in control. What happened. Just like Cali said about herself, she was talking about me, also, and didn't know it. Does sex rule our lives now? I need to go back and see Leland and Linda, where I can get my bearings again.*

The trip was long and Kelly had time to think. He was now at a cross road of his life. He had thought that Cali was the woman he would spend his life with. He now didn't know. The opium had done a job on her. It had lowered her morals until she wanted something to replace the opium and that was sex. She had admitted she liked the things that the guards did to her. She didn't know he had witnessed it, and thought he understood it was Estabon, but it wasn't. After the men had used her, she thought she liked it. It was the opium that had changed her. She now didn't know who she was. She needed some time to herself. She needed to sort things out. Someone who had such control of herself had been violently shook. People who are the most confident, can be shook to their toes when they lose control, and let their urges control them. That was what Cali had done. She had lost control, because of the opium. She needed love when they were in Savanna, and he sent her away, and wasn't there for her. The handsome stranger was. She had just reached out for love, and he wasn't there, but the stranger was. She also wanted to hurt him, because he wasn't there.

Kelly then wondered about what she said about the next morning. She was stone sober, but still wanted the man's sex. That he didn't understand. She knew what she was doing, and still wanted the man's sex in the worst way. It was like slapping him in the face. He could understand what she did the night before, but the next morning when she knew what she was doing, she wanted the man.

He had heard of women who had been sexually exploited at a young age. They succumbed to their need for sex at first not through their will, but later, they needed sex to feel wanted. That made some women insatiable.

Kelly reached Leland's ranch and was glad to be there. Linda hugged him first, just a short hug. Then he hugged Leland and began to cry. He needed Leland as he would have his dad. Leland and Linda could tell he had been under terrific stress. Leland held him tight and said, "It's okay, Son. You're home now with the people who love you. We will make you well again."

"They walked into the house and Linda poured him a brandy. Kelly didn't say a word, he just drank the brandy, then asked for more. He had drank several ounces before he looked up.

Kelly said, "My wife was kidnapped and taken to Cuba. I spent a lot of time getting her back. I didn't realize the stress she went through. When we returned, we took a trip to Savanna, Georgia. It was very nice there. After two days I was offered a job. I was offered ten thousand dollars to take the job.

I didn't realize how deeply the kidnapping had affected Cali. I told her that the job was dangerous, and that she needed to return to Boston. The job wasn't dangerous, but the person hiring me was a beautiful woman.

She returned to New York City by ship and met a handsome man aboard. She needed to escape so she drank a lot. She ended up in the man's cabin and slept with him. When she awoke she was a different person. She told me about it, and said she wanted and needed the man's sex. I told her that I understood, and that she only did what nearly anyone would do under the circumstances. However, she could not forgive me or herself. She said she didn't know if she could stay true to me. She wanted sometime to be alone. As she put it, she needed some space to think out what had happened to her, and where she would go from there.

"I figured she had lost her love for me during her affair with the man. She didn't know where she was or where she would end up. The only thing she knew was that she didn't want me around her.

"I left and didn't look back. I don't know if I will ever see her again, or want to. She killed something in me, just like I killed something in her, when I sent her away when she wasn't over the terrible trauma. The man who kidnapped her used her like a whore. She was made to do things she didn't want to do to a man she hated. I didn't understand that or I would have never taken the job in Savanna.

"The job paid ten thousand dollars and I only did five days work to collect it. However, I would give a hundred thousand to have passed up that job. It cost me my wife and her love for me, and maybe my love for her."

Leland excused himself to answer a call of nature.

After he left, Linda broke the silence by saying, "You need a long rest with the people who love you the most. Sleep late and go to work with Leland. He has a way to soothe you by just being with him. I never knew love. Leland has changed my life so much, I can't explain it. I knew the first time I saw him, that he was different from the other men I had known. He took a homely dancehall girl, who has laid with more men that you can count, and gave her the love she never had. I love him with every fiber of my body. He loves you like he did his first wife and Patty. He told me he loves you like the son he never had.

"He once said, 'Let's pretend he's our son, Lynda. Let's treasure the time he spends with us.'"

Leland returned and said, "Let's get some sleep."

Kelly slept deeply for the first time in years. He was home. When he was in town after two weeks, He checked his mail and there was a card from Colonel Alfred that asked him to report to Langley. He returned a card that said he was on his way.

He promised to write, and they both hugged him before he got on his horse. He stopped in Joplin for the night. He bathed changed clothes and had dinner. He then went to the saloon that Betty Kelly owned. He walked in as she was about to walk out and she came into his arms and they kissed a long kiss.

Betty then said, "I'll be back in a minute. Order us a brandy."

When she returned they drank their drink and she said, "Come to my room and bring that bottle."

He told Betty a cut down version of his past year. He also said his wife had told him to give her some space as she needed to have time to sort things out.

Betty said, "I plan to fill some of that space. After making love to you, I realize you make love better than anyone. You take your time and make a girl feel she is special. I like that, and I bet every woman you have laid, feels the same way. I don't mind being the girl in the port of Joplin as long as you visit that port once in awhile."

"I don't want to offend you, Betty, but I'm not ready to be with you. I have to sort some things out. Maybe the next time I come through. I know I told you we are apart, but I have to make sure of that before I can bed you. Do you understand?"

"Yes, and I admire you for it. As much as I want you, I want your welfare more. If you love her, you should return to her."

CHAPTER 21

THE CALL TO ALASKA

The next morning at breakfast Kelly told her he had an assignment, and must leave. It took another eight days to reach Langley. Colonel Alfred said, "I have a special assignment for you, Marshal Andrews. As you know, America purchased Alaska on March 30, 1867.

"However, there are Russians who live there and do not recognize the purchase. They think they own the portion of land that they live on. They have killed Americans, and other people to enforce what they think is their right to the property on the island of Sitka.

"You are to go to Sitka, and let the Russians know that America is in charge and they are to return to Russia if they don't like it."

"This appears to be an assignment for the Army. Why not send in our troops and give them a real lesson?"

"The president doesn't want to inflame the Russian Government. He wants this handled in a low key manner. I thought of you, because you are good at putting bullies in their place.

Before Kelly left DC, he wrote a letter to Cali. It said:

Dear Cali,

I still love you. I wish I had just spent some time with you, so we could have talked it all out. I believe the opium made you do the things you did. It controlled your thought patternto the point you lost control of everything.

You needed me in Savanna and I sent you away You were so vulnerable you could not control your actions. I abandoned you when you needed me the most. I hate myself for that. I told Leland and Linda that I earned ten thousand dollars in five day and lost the love of my life in doing so. I would now give a million dollars to have not sent you away. If we have lost our love, it's my fault. We had a precious thing and I ruined it.

Love, Kelly

Kelly mailed the letter and then caught the a train to New York City and from Union Station, bought a ticket to San Francisco. When he was aboard the train he began thinking again. He felt terrible about their situation. There are some things that cannot be undone once they happen. He wondered if this was one of them. He thought of his indiscretions with sex. Sex was a terrible thing when misused. He could now see that sex, when used like God intended, was a wonderful thing that God blessed, but when misused, it brought only guilt and bad feelings. Cali was probably like that now. The opium had broken down all her inhibitions. She had lost control of herself. He wondered if he had also. He wished they were together, so they could talk out what they felt.

He thought, *"If a man can keep control of his sex life, then he probably can control the other sins that confront him."*

He then thought of all the men he had killed. *"Sure, they were outlaws and the enemy, but why would he kill them? Over money he was paid? Ideology, that surely wasn't much of a reason. He again thought how he had changed. He was just like Cali. It had not been a drug that changed him. He had changed himself. He was now on another mission where he would undoubtedly kill again, and why? Some men had owned that land most of their lives, and thought it was theirs forever. Maybe they were right."*

He was now thirty miles out of New York City. He got off at the next stop, and caught the next train back to New York City.

Cali had just read his letter. She was crying and love poured over her as it had when she first saw Kelly in Houston. She remembered his eyes, Cooper's eyes, had beguiled her.

About that time the front door opened, and there stood Kelly. She flew into his arms, and held him so tightly he could barely breath.

He said, "We can make it, honey, we can make it!

THE END

Printed in the United States
By Bookmasters